Key of the PROPHECY

An Ellen Thompson Thriller

By Vicki Williamson

ISBN-13: 978-0-9990605-0-6

To my sons, Joshua and Zachary.
You are my heart and pride.

CONTENTS

Chapter 1

The soft click of the door as it slides shut behind me centers my attention. In the quiet, the only sounds are my breathing and the steady beat of my heart. My training has become second nature and my focus is absolute.

The little house is dimly lit. The windows are boarded, and the only light comes through the cracks around each plank. It streaks across the room in places, which obscures my vision as dust motes dance like fairies in the still air. It's silent. Eerily silent.

I scan the room through the front sight of my favorite weapon—she's a Heckler & Koch-VP9 and fits like a well-worn glove. With my gun kept at eye level and my arms slightly bent, I duck walk heel-to-toe through the room, sweeping left and right, looking for any threat.

Advancing through the room, I'm attuned to every nuance of sound, smell, and motion. As I round the corner of the hallway, a silhouette springs out. I pivot and pull the trigger. My gun kicks as the slide jacks backward, expelling a shell and the acrid sting of smoke, but I'm already moving. Down the hall and around the corner, in the kitchen, is another encounter. My training and instincts are fluid as my gun cracks. Every time it sounds, my calm becomes deeper, my breath smoother, and my heartbeat steadier.

Something swings from the ceiling and I react, almost shooting, but at the last second, I stop. Friendly—no threat here. Stepping to the side, I continue to the back of the house. The rear door is visible; this is almost finished. *Don't get ahead of yourself, El. Calm, cool, and collected. Keep your head. You've got this.*

Moving down the hallway, I'm hit in the shoulder and knocked into the wall. I tuck my legs and roll to the side to avoid a second hit. Up on one foot and a knee, peering back, I take the shot.

Back on my feet and moving, in just two more steps I'm through the doorway and into the sun and warmth. With a quick motion, I holster my weapon and slide my ear and eye protection off as I'm lifted in a mighty bear hug. I can't help but laugh as I'm swung around and set back gently on the ground.

"Great job, Ellen! You absolutely rocked the course, and

that was your best time yet!"

I look up at my firearms instructor, Mac Sullivan. I'm tall for a woman, but when I say I look up—I mean I look *up*. Mac's a former Navy Seal, and he's a mountain of a man. Right now, he has a huge smile on his affable face, a smile that makes me grin back. We've become good friends, and his opinion of me means the world.

I give him a wry smile and a tilt of my head. "Thanks, Mac. I owe it all to your expert tutelage."

"Now El, don't sell yourself short. Passion and practice, I always say—and you have truckloads of both."

He reaches out, and we connect with a fist bump that's all about comradery.

Finishing with the live fire exercise, and after a short visit with Mac, I head home. It's an hour drive, and my mind fills with thoughts of the past and the worry I've felt all week. It's been a little over a year since my life and story truly began in France. Even though I've put what happened with James and the Poppies behind me, my sense of wariness and betrayal linger.

After those experiences, I couldn't return to Michigan and didn't want to stay in Europe. I tried to return to my normal life, truly. Even went back to work at the Detroit Institute of Art, but I couldn't focus, couldn't be that same person. Funny how love, loss, and death will do that to a girl.

So, I moved on. Art is still my first love, and I couldn't give that up, not with the loss of everything else. My position at the DIA took hard work to achieve, but I soon realized downsizing was the answer. The Phoenix Art Museum was the perfect choice. Topographically, my life is different—I mean, Michigan to Arizona? Culture shock is putting it mildly. But I'm in love with Arizona. Where else can it be over ninety degrees and only a short drive to the mountains? Phoenix is the perfect size. It's a big city, but still feels down-home. The dry air and heat agree with me. I even sold my old Toyota and bought a Jeep.

One good thing, a great thing, to come out of France was a new friendship. Adrien Bernard, a French cop who was there when I desperately needed someone, has become very dear to my heart—fatherly, beloved. We're half a world apart, but with modern technology, we're able to stay close. We usually touch base every day, at least every other. But recently, it's been four days of nothing. I've even attempted to call him. On the drive home, one of my favorite Talk Radio channels is on, but I keep losing track of the conversation, and then I almost take a wrong turn getting to my house. My mind is flitting around, unable to concentrate. I'm worried.

*****

My name is Ellen Thompson and my story has changed.

When I arrive at my house, I can't help but notice how different my existence has become. In Michigan, my home was a fourth-floor apartment—now in Arizona I rent a cute townhome. Here, I have a yard, though it's gravel and cactus with a couple of Arizona yellow bells—flowering shrubs that are even more beautiful backed by the simplicity of the desert.

As I enter my house, I place my bag and range case on the kitchen table. With a quick look, my eyes scan my home. I was able to salvage some of my collection of artwork and antiques when I left Michigan, items that withstood the break-in and break-up of my apartment. They're kept in places of honor, as the satisfaction of a hunt for new treasures has soured. Among others, there's an old hardbound book with a bronze locking mechanism, a single china teacup with a rose motif, and a little bit of whimsy in a ceramic rooster with a large red comb.

I'll clean and lock the gun in a moment, but first, I want to try to contact Adrien. My laptop fires up, and I log onto Skype, hearing its distinctive signature tone. Selecting Adrien's contact, I hit enter. While it rings, I hurry to the fridge to grab a bottled water and then hustle back to the table to watch as Adrien doesn't answer.

"Damn it, Adrien! Where the hell are you?"

After a few moments of listless ringing, I discontinue the attempt but leave my Skype account open in case he tries me. As I get dinner and prepare for bed, I decide if he doesn't contact me by tomorrow, I'll contact his work.

Chapter 2

"No, ma'am. Yes, ma'am. Adrien Bernard. Yes, Detective Adrien Bernard...

"What do you mean there's no Detective Bernard employed there? Of course there is." An immediate headache spikes through my eye at her continued insistence. With a hard rub at my temple, I pace my living room.

"Ma'am, I'm sorry, but I know Detective Adrien Bernard works there. He's in his late fifties, gray hair, bearded face...he may have taken some time off. How long have you worked there? Can you check with someone else?" I pull my cell phone from my ear as the woman breaks into a tirade of angry French and hangs up. "What the hell?" I mutter with a shake of my head, and stare at my phone in confusion. *What's going on?*

*****

All day, my phone call to the National Police in Paris occupies my thoughts. What was with that conversation? What did she mean, "no Adrien Bernard works here?" Unable to complete any work, my mind returns again and again to Adrien. Where is he? I text him several times as the day progresses, but to no avail. It's been five days now, and I don't know what to do. Is he in trouble? He was there for me, helped me, and supported me when those things were needed the most. I can't—won't— let him go without a fight. I have to know what's happening.

The next day's the same. I wander around pretending to get work done but keep looking at my phone. *Where are you, Adrien? How can I help when I don't know what's going on?*

By the time the sun sets on the sixth day, I wonder if I've lost my mind. Have I read too much into this? Is there even something to be worried about?

After sitting on my patio to watch the sun shrink behind the horizon, I head into the house to attempt to get a good night's sleep. Maybe it'll all look different in the morning. Just as I head to the stairs, there's a knock on the door. *Kinda late, but okay…*

It's dark outside. Peering through the peephole, I see the

outline of a man's back. With a cautious move, I open the door but keep the screen locked until finding out who and what this visit entails. The man turns, and although his face is distorted by the exterior light hitting the metal of the screen, I'd know him anywhere.

"*Adrien!*" With a yell, I yank open the door to throw myself at him. He catches me and wraps me in a parental hug.

"Ellen. Step inside, please." He's subdued and wary. He scans left and right, scenting the air like a hunted animal, his eyes moving over every shadow.

"Of course, of course. Where have you been? What are you doing here?"

"Let's go in. I'll explain what I can."

As we walk into the house, he almost trips, making me realize how unsteady he is. His hand on my arm is less about an attempt to direct me and more about keeping himself upright.

Looking closer, I feel a pang of worry. It's obvious he's weak. His face has little color and he looks shrunken. "Adrien, are you all right? Can I get you something to drink or eat?"

I steer him to a kitchen chair and don't let go of him until he's seated. In a squat before him, I take his hand in mine. It's cold and clammy. Questions run rampant through my brain and I search for something to do.

"What can I get you? What can I do for you? Please, let me help you."

With a shaky, wispy breath, he says, "We must be quick, but a glass of water would be most welcome, my dear."

Anxious to do something, anything, I grab a glass from the cupboard and fill it with water. I sit back on my haunches and help him take a drink. His hands shake badly.

"What do you mean, 'we must be quick?' Quick to do what?"

As he finishes his swallow, he sets the glass down. He peers at me intently and then surprises me when he reaches out and lifts my medallion from my collarbone. I sit still as he stares at it, rubbing his thumb along its surface. As if he's come to a decision, he drops the necklace and looks me in the eye.

"Get packed." Adrien's gaze is direct, unflinching. It's a look I've never seen before, and prickles finger up my spine. "We need to leave immediately."

I shake my head. "What are you talking about, Adrien? I'm not going anywhere. And I don't think you could if you wanted. You need to rest."

He grasps me by the upper arm, surprising me with his strength. As he stands, he pulls me with. "Get a bag. We're leaving *now*."

"What's going on? Where are we going?"

"I'll tell you as we go. Right now, we have to move." There's a pleading in his eyes. "Please, Ellen. Please, trust me."

"All right, Adrien. All right. Just give me ten minutes."

"Quickly. As quick as you can. I don't know how much time we have."

He sits but looks at me expectantly. With one last, confused look, I hurry to my room. First things first, I grab my holster and open the safe, which holds my gun. The weapon is kept as home defense, so it's loaded, with one in the chamber—ready to rock. I put the gun in the holster and hook it to my belt.

After the turmoil of last year and the move to Arizona, I

took a good look at my life and the dangers that are around every corner. I started with self-defense lessons. It began innocently enough. There was an ad for an all-women's class in the local paper, and I couldn't get it out of my head. It might have come in handy last year, and what could it hurt? So, I went. I stood in the back, a little embarrassed, if I'm honest. But I watched and listened and signed up for the full course. After that, I signed up again, and then later for a more advanced course. One day, I found myself researching firearms. I tried one out and bought it. I guess it's a slippery slope to self-reliance and self-protection. And when I met Mac Sullivan, there was no going back.

With a hurried step, I enter my walk-in closet and grab a tote from the corner. On a shelf in the back is a small personal safe that holds important papers and money. Part of the overall emergency plan is cash. It'll work unless there's a world war or a zombie apocalypse, and I just don't have the initiative to plan for that, so cash will have to do.

I grab my entire life's savings — four bundles of twenties, $10,000 worth — and stick them in the bottom of my bag. Surprisingly, they take up very little room. In the back of the safe, my gaze catches on something, and figuring better safe than sorry, I reach in, grab my passport, and toss it in the bag. With a stretch to a high shelf, I grab a few boxes of ammunition. A couple moments more to grab a clean pair of jeans, changes of underwear, random T-shirts, and a jacket, and I'm ready to go. My purse joins everything else in my tote so I'll have less to carry.

When I return, Adrien is still at the table. He's slumped and a surge of panic hits me. With a quick step, I rush to his side, drop my bag, and stoop to grasp his shoulder. He jerks and half-rises from the chair.

"Jesus, Adrien. You about gave me a heart attack," I mumble under my breath.

"You're ready?" He looks me over. "Leave your cell phone."

"What? What *are* you talking about? This is crazy!"

"Your cell can be tracked."

"Tracked?" I ask him. "How did you even get here?"

"I took the bus and then walked. I wasn't followed."

"Followed by whom?" Is he delusional? Maybe he's sick and this is evidence of its effect.

"Ellen...I told you. You'll have to trust me. Now we must be—"

All of a sudden, the world shifts. There's a flash of reflected light outside, a window breaks, and I'm on the floor with Adrien lying over me. He's knocked me to the ground with surprisingly agile reflexes. There're two more explosions as another pane of glass shatters. A high-pitched wail comes from all around us and it's only after a moment I realize the sound is emanating from within my ears. Dimly, as if he's talking over an old-time phone line, I hear Adrien's voice.

"*Bon sang!* They've found us! Where is your vehicle?" His gaze flies around the kitchen.

With a shake of my head to clear it, I roll to look at him. "Found us? Who found us?"

"Your vehicle, Ellen! Quit asking questions and let's go!"

The sound of a car outside pushes me into gear as I hear it screech to a stop.

"The garage is through here," I say and point to the hallway. "My Jeep is in the garage."

Adrien grabs my arm with one hand and my bag with

the other. He stays crouched and rushes us across the kitchen and down the hallway. He slows by the garage door, let's go of my arm, and shoves my bag at me. I automatically take it from him. Door cracked, he peers in and then around the edge into the garage. The light is off, it's quiet, and — other than the vehicle — vacant. He opens the door and pulls me after him.

"Where are your keys?"

I drop my tote and open it to grab my purse. With a quick rifle through, I find my keys. Adrien grabs them from my hand.

"Hey!" I say crossly.

"Get in. I'll drive."

He opens the back door and throws my tote in. Before I realize it, he's in the driver's seat and peering at me with an expectant and impatient look.

With a mental shrug, I rush to climb into the front passenger seat. A car door slams, and I hear the faded sound of voices — men's voices.

Adrien reaches into an interior pocket of his jacket. He pulls out a small device, which he plugs into the cigarette lighter.

"What's that?"

"Put on your seat belt, Ellen," he says and fastens his.

I grab my belt and strap myself in.

Adrien sits motionless. He hasn't put the key in the ignition, hasn't started the Jeep, and isn't opening the garage. For a man in such a hurry, he seems pretty happy to sit still.

"Adrien," I begin.

"Shh…"

I quiet and realize he's listening. With that thought in my head, I'm hyper-sensitive and strain to hear every sound.

My heart is beating so fast and hard it's pounding in my throat.

Adrien puts the key in the ignition and waits. There's a loud crash as my front door is breeched and the sound of raised voices comes to us through the hall. Adrien reacts. He turns the key and kicks over the engine. Throwing the Jeep into reverse, he backs out, crashing straight through the garage door.

With a shriek of surprise and disbelief, I grab the car door with one hand, the dash with the other. As we roar backward down the driveway, we bounce and jostle over pieces of my garage door. In the street, Adrien performs a perfect turn, stop, and start, and we accelerate away. Men run from my house into the street to watch us go. In the light of the dashboard, I stare at Adrien with speculation. He handles the Jeep like Mario Andretti. Apparently, there are depths to this man I know nothing about.

Chapter 3

Slumped in the lumpy, smelly hotel chair, I watch Adrien sleep. I may never sleep again.

Soon after we left my condo in such a flurry, Adrien and I changed seats. He was in no condition to drive, especially after the adrenaline of our escape wore off. When I questioned him about my Jeep being tracked by GPS, he informed me the object he plugged into the cigarette lighter was a jammer.

"What do you mean?" I asked.

Out of the corner of my eye, I saw him watch me as he

indicated the small device. "The jammer will stop any signals from this vehicle."

"Jammer, huh?" I muttered and gave my attention to the road. What was this? A James Bond movie?

When we were certain—at least as much as we could be—that we weren't being followed, with or without a jammer, I quit making random road and lane changes. I wasn't sure where we were and knew Adrien wasn't either. We'd moved through a few small towns—towns I didn't even know existed—and now I've pulled into this little hole-in-the-wall motel to give myself time to come up with some kind of plan. The aimless driving was making me crazed.

I got us a room in the back and barely got Adrien in before he collapsed on the bed. I've sat here, with my gun in my hand, for hours. He's dead to the world, and I can't leave him—not even to get food. My eyes are scratchy, and my body feels twitchy and achy, but I can't relax. Who were those men? Maybe I should force Adrien up and keep going. But going to where? My life is in turmoil. I don't know what's happening and where my sane existence went. Who is this man? It's obvious he's not who I thought he was.

It's a moment later—or is it hours? I can't sit and worry for another instant. I need answers. I'm a pacer by nature, but my fatigue is so heavy I can't force myself out of the chair. My skin is crawling and itchy, and although I'm exhausted, I keep shifting in an attempt to locate a comfortable position. I'm about to wake Adrien when his breathing changes and his body shifts. I straighten with attention, watching as he rouses. His eyes are foggy and he mutters, "Ellen."

I stare at him but don't answer.

With a groan, he sits on the bed and swings his legs over

the side. He sighs and straightens his back to stand gingerly. With a glance around the room, he says, "How long have we been here? We must keep moving."

"Where, Adrien? Where are we going? *Why* are we going?"

"I'll explain, but later—now we have to leave."

I shake my head and sit forward with my elbows on my knees; my gun is still in my hand hanging toward the floor. I want to go, I need to go, but I need answers more. "No. Now. Right now. You're going to tell me why men broke into my house, why you crashed my vehicle out of my garage, why we're on the run, and *who the hell you even are*." The last part I say with a near shout, and I'm startled by my hysterical tone. With a deep breath, I calm myself, excusing the outburst, putting it down to shock, exhaustion, and hunger. But, although Adrien looks at me with forced patience, I'm ready to stand my ground.

"Ellen..."

I shake my head again. I'm not moving.

Resigned, he sits on the end of the bed. "Tell me what you remember about your medallion."

"What?" Of all the things I expected, this wasn't it.

"Your medallion." He inclines his head, his eyes on my necklace.

I touch the bronze piece. It's familiar—like an old friend. It was a gift from my parents. They were killed in a car accident a little over ten years ago, and I never take it off.

"Tell me about it."

I explain how my parents gave me the necklace as a surprise one day—quite out of the blue, really. I've always been enamored with antiques, and this emblem is amazing.

It's about the size of a fifty-cent piece, with a hole in the middle. It has varied symbols all around and on the reverse side. It's quite unique. My mother said she saw it and knew it was mine. Since that day, it's become a part of me.

"Did you ever question the markings?" He seems tired but reconciled to this discussion. I have a sense of foreboding and suddenly wish I'd never pushed us into this conversation.

"They're old. Egyptian maybe."

"Older still," he mutters softly, and my stomach twists as a spike of adrenaline hits my system. With a deep breath, he tells a story of what my medallion represents. I listen about past civilizations, varied and around the world. A primary symbol, a symbol used by many, is represented by my medallion. He digs in the bedside dresser for paper and a pen and draws a symbol. It's a cross with the ends bent at ninety degree angles.

"A swastika? Are you insane? You're saying my parents were *Nazis*?" I push myself out of the chair and past him. I slide my gun in my belt and grab my bags.

"Ellen, wait." Adrien stands and grabs my arm. "Listen to me."

With a jerk, I tear my arm from his hold. Turning on him, I jab my finger in his face and yell, "You didn't even know my parents. They were amazing people. I'm not going to stand here and let you disparage their memories, not to me." I snatch the car keys and head for the door. I'm out of here.

"Ellen, *Sacrebleu!* Listen to me. The swastika wasn't always a representation of Nazi Germany. For eons, it's been used by many people, ancient people. It means good fortune." He grabs my arm again and spins me around. "Are you

17

listening? This has nothing to do with Nazis." With an earnest look, begging for understanding, he begins to speak in a sing-song voice, his words in a rhythm, like an old familiar tune I can't quite place.

"Down through the ages, past eons untold,
the elders stand watch — never to change, never grow old."

Blinking rapidly, I stare at him, my brows pulled together. Why is he talking in rhyme? And it sounds so familiar.

"Destined to merely witness, powerless to inspire or sway,
man's existence gifted with free-will, due to choices, may he stray."

"Adrien. What are you saying?"

He stares at me and, as if I hadn't spoken, he continues.

As he speaks, a shiver runs up my back and a buzz begins on the top of my head and spills over like water running from my crown. I want to shut him up, but I'm held spellbound by his words—words that resonate in my head. Foreign yet familiar.

"Tradition and lore are inspired, through stories told from the past.
The elders seen as spirits, as helpful aides they have been cast."

Without a conscious thought, I join him in the rhythm of the poem, our voices sounding as one in the close interior of the hotel room.

"Now the cycle comes 'round, a calling once again made,
a new Guardian foretold, the ultimate offering to be paid.

Guidance is imparted. Use of the Key will ease the way.
The elders' challenge accepted, an age-old game is now in play."

The sound of our voices seems to hang in the air, even after we stop speaking.

"What was that?" I stare at Adrien. My breathing is rapid, and my body breaks into a cold sweat. I feel as though I've been possessed by someone or something. As if I'm watching us from afar.

"When, as a young child, you began to exhibit traits...traits which few possess, traits which are stronger within you than any of us could have fathomed, your parents contacted me. They were worried what it might mean for you, for your future. But, also excited that you might be the one we've waited for. The one the prophecy speaks of — the Key.

"Truthfully, your family had become my family, and I would stop at nothing to aid them. I used all my contacts to get information. To discover what was happening to you. But, suddenly, you stopped developing. We didn't know you deliberately tramped these talents down. Had we known, we might have helped you in your confusion."

Backtracking, I say, "The one you waited for? The Key?" My hand is at my throat, rubbing. I look down to find myself stroking my medallion. Breathing is difficult, as if my throat is closing off. This day has been full of shocks, and my mind can't take much more. "And what was with that poem, that song?" I speak quietly, almost afraid to hear his answer, yet my voice has a shrill quality that rings out in the confined space.

"Ellen," Adrien says with patience in his tone. "You're Ellen. You'll always be Ellen." He reaches out and takes my hand to squeeze lightly. "You're perfect and beautiful." With a warm glance, he runs his hand down my hair. "I think the discussion of the prophecy should be kept for another time, another place."

"Prophecy?"

"Our discussion should start at the beginning, *vous ne pensez pas*? Let's step back and talk about your parents and your medallion."

I look at him, at this once trusted, beloved face. I want to trust him again, maybe even need to trust him. I drop my belongings and resume my seat in the chair. "Tell me."

A small, sad smile crosses his lips, and his eyes lose focus as he looks over my shoulder. "David and Mary Thompson," he says with a shake of his head, folding his hands. "I met your parents in Paris at a book reading of an author we admired. They were in France on holiday. After the reading, there was a meet-and-greet where we chanced to stand together and visit with some interesting, influential people. I recall the discussion was one on the origins of man's stories—a thought-provoking subject. I looked up to catch your father's eye. It seemed we were kindred spirits.

"We met later and then again, many times. We had the same questions. Why did so many past and present civilizations around the globe have the same stories and use the same symbols? They existed at different times and in different places, yet the symbols—in particular, the swastika— were universally used, revered, and even had the same meaning.

"Then dear Mary discovered she was pregnant with you, and it was that which pushed them in their quest to find something better, some answer to their questions. We believed, and I still believe, that our histories, our mythologies stem from a more tangible source. We met with others who held the same ideas. Others who did not always maintain the same ethical standards as us, however. Some of these people split from the group — they called themselves the Guild; they are the reason your parents left Paris, why they returned to America before you were born."

With a pause, he drops his head to study his hands and then looking at me again, his eyes sparkle. "I was a little in love with her, myself — your mother. It was hard not to be. You knew her later, but at the time of your birth she was not only as loving and funny as always, but more carefree. Everyone adored her and your father. Their death was a tragedy." Adrien walks toward the rear of the room. He turns and gazes at me. "We maintained our friendship through the years and when we met again, it was as if we were never apart. Over time, we became friends with other individuals who looked for their own answers. The medallion and the history of the prophecy was what we found — our guidebook."

My mind is in a swirl with all this information. Standing, I begin to pace in the small room. "How did you find me last year in Paris? You were a police officer, but the National Police has no record of you."

"No, Ellen. I'm sorry for the subterfuge. It was necessary to help you reach safety but keep you out of the spotlight. I'm not an officer of the National Police, but I have contacts with many state agencies and foreign governments. I'm here to protect you and be an aid in this quest we are to undertake and along the road it will lead us upon."

"Why me, Adrien? What makes me special?"

"The puzzle begins and ends with your medallion. The

faith of the group held that there was one person who could pull it all together. One person, a Key, who would solve the mystery and find the location of the Guardian. The medallion is much like a map, laying a path before us. And it chose you. We must trust and follow that path, decipher it. But we must be careful. When I was attacked recently in Paris, I realized there is an unsavory element after the same information. I believe it to be the Guild — the group your parents and I separated from for…ethical reasons. They haven't changed at all. In possession of the Guardian, they think they can rule the world. I believe it was their men at your home."

Don't mad men always want to rule the world? Adrien evaded them and made his way to America, but he was almost too late. They arrived at my house on his tail.

"I need you with me, Ellen. We must follow the clues, put together the puzzle, and figure out the path of the Key — your path. When the path is known, it will lead to the Guardian and the cycle will be fulfilled."

"What is this Guardian?"

With a small shake of his head, Adrien says, "All we know are the words of the prophecy. A new Guardian is foretold and the Key will find him. The only information we have been given, through the ages of time, is we need to start with the Hopi Indians. We need to travel to the Hopi village of Oraibi and follow the medallion."

"Follow the medallion, okay. But it's safe to say we're being tracked."

"Yes, but I believe we've lost them for now. As we get closer to Oraibi and our quest begins, I'm sure we'll encounter them again. We'll need to take precautions and be quick."

My brow furrows. "Precautions." I nod my head in

agreement, thinking furiously.

Continuing his thought, Adrien adds, "A change in vehicles and perhaps a disguise of our appearances. If we are swift and not obvious, we may continue to evade them. A few towns back we passed a small used car lot. It's the middle of the night but we need to keep moving. We've been stationary too long as it is. Come morning, we'll make a trade for your Jeep."

"Trade my Jeep? Do you really think that's necessary?" At his nod, I mutter, "I love my Jeep. Where is this village of Oraibi?"

"After we switch vehicles, we'll head northeast for about four hours."

"And what happens when we get there?"

"I have a contact we will get in touch with. She'll be our guide and get us into the village. After that..." With a shrug and a smile Adrien gives me an adventurous look. "I suggest we see when we arrive."

Chapter 4

With a tank full of gas and food for the trip, we're ready. My eyes feel as if they've been sprinkled with sand and my attention is drifting, but fuel is necessary, so I dine on a microwave burrito and raspberry tea. A half-smile crosses my face as Adrien reacts to his fare. He's driving one-handed and eating his own gourmet sample from the gas station; gulping American coffee, he decrees, "*Atroce.*"

We head back the way we came and pass the used car lot. It's dark, but morning is fast approaching. We'll soon be able to speak with someone about a change of vehicle.

I've hardly had any sleep in the past twenty-four hours,

and it's making me feel a bit addled. My brain is mush.

Adrien pulls onto a dark, quiet side street and turns off the engine. He pushes his seat back and lays it down. With his arms folded, he looks as if he's going to take a nap. *How can he relax?*

Through a partially cracked window, I hear the songs of birds as they begin their welcome to the sun. This time of morning is my favorite — it has such promise. What will our day bring?

"Adrien?" I ask. "Can you tell me more of what led you here? What we can expect in the village?"

With his eyes closed and his body relaxed, Adrien speaks. "The village of Old Oraibi is a step back in time. The Hopi people have chosen to forsake modern conveniences and live like their ancestors. We'll look for the swastika symbol — it's used by certain kachina or spirits. The Hopi people have many ceremonial dances where kachina costumes are worn. Kachina, the costumes, and kachina dolls are very important in Hopi society."

"Dolls? Like Barbie or Raggedy Ann?"

In the dim light of morning, the corners of his mouth turn up in a small smile. "No, Ellen. The kachina dolls are a teaching tool for the Hopi children. A way to learn the different helping spirits and know they're always with you. The Hopi believe all things have a spirit: animals, rocks, rain, everything — people, too. Some kachina help with growing corn, some help with receiving rain, and some keep people on the correct religious path.

"The Hopi prophecies foretell the return of Pahana, or the True White Brother — we would call him God. When Pahana returns, he'll be accompanied by two helpers. One of his helpers is represented by the swastika. Because of this, the symbol is sacred and used in religious ceremonies. It is this we will look for."

I nod my understanding, but my eyes are heavy with sleep. As I drift off, my head is filled with spirits, symbols, and questions.

When the engine turns over, my eyes open in puzzlement. *Where am I?* With a swing of my head, I recognize the interior of my Jeep. We're heading back to town.

"Good morning, *ma chère.*"

"Adrien." With my seat once again in an upright position, I look out the window. The houses are well tended, and a few of them have grass, though most are gravel-and-cactus landscaping. We're only a few blocks from the main highway and the car lot. I already miss my Jeep.

*****

When we pull out of the used car lot in a later-model Honda, I'm sure the part-time salesman and his manager are high-fiving each other with glee. They certainly got the better of this trade. Before we leave town, Adrien pulls into a convenience store. He hurries in, and within a few moments, he's back. He puts two bags in the backseat.

"What's that?"

"Some items we will need."

Questions push to get out past my lips, but I stay silent. Do I even want to know what we'll do at this point? What I want is some space to think. It'll be about four hours until we reach the village of Oraibi. Keyed up, but still exhausted, it

26

seems there's no way to get some more rest. Thoughts on how weird that combination of emotions is fill my mind as I drift off.

*****

The slowing of the Honda wakes me. With a rub of my eyes and a jaw-popping yawn, I give a stretch that fills the seat. "Are we there?"

"This is Tuba City, the nearest accommodation to Oraibi. We should find a hotel, make our preparations for tomorrow, and get some rest. We'll head to Old Oraibi in the morning. It's forty-five miles east."

With a nod, I agree. Exhaustion sits heavy on me, even having slept. The nap wasn't restful; it was full of dreams that are hard to remember. Adrien pulls into a small motel, and we get a room in the back with a view of the offices and the highway.

"I hope you don't mind the necessity of one room. I believe it will be safer if we stay together."

With a shake of my head, I say, "Of course. I'm fine with the accommodations and I'll feel better having you close."

When we walk into our room, I drop my bag on the farthest bed and glance around. It'll do. It's modest and dated, but clean. The downtime will help me get centered and ready for what's to come, whatever that might be.

Adrien enters behind me and shuts and locks the door. He walks to the bed, where he upends the grocery bags from the convenience shop. Scattered on the spread with other items are razors, hair color, and a package of scissors.

With a resigned sigh, I turn to face Adrien. "So what are we doing?"

"It will be prudent to alter our appearance. I fear we are being closely trailed and we don't want to make their job any easier."

"Okay. What do I do?"

*****

The shower feels amazing. Quaint place, but the water is hot, the pressure high. The in-room soaps are coarse and smell harsh—like lye and pine—but I'm clean. Getting out of the shower and wrapped in a short scratchy towel, I step to the sink. With a swipe of my hand, I wipe the condensation from the mirror and look at my reflection. Staring back at me is a woman I don't recognize. She's in her thirties and pretty, but instead of long, slightly wavy brunette hair, she has a short black crop. Reaching up, my fingers feather through the strands and I note even my face looks fuller. My eyes, instead of hazel, appear green.

In a shift of the light, a spark catches my eye and I see my medallion reflecting where it lies on my collarbone. It's luminous in the bright and slightly harsh bathroom lighting. As I spin around to lean against the sink, I reach to unhook the chain from my throat. With the medallion in my palm, I examine it closely. I've always liked the piece, not only because it was a gift from my parents but because from the first moment, I felt it was mine—had always been mine.

The medallion fills my palm, and with the hole in the middle, it's always reminded me of foreign money. There are different symbols on it—some look like the letter L set at

28

different angles, there are curly Qs, and even what looks like Asian writing. I've never concerned myself with what the symbols meant; they just were. Now, however, the nuances of every line and etching stand out. I shrug and allow myself the luxury of not knowing everything tonight.

Returning the necklace to its place on my neck, I towel dry, brush the snarls from my hair, and hang the damp towel over the shower rod. After tossing on a T-shirt and shorts to sleep in, I walk back into the hotel room. Adrien sits by the window, with a small portion of the drape folded back, watching the parking lot and the highway.

He turns to gaze at me and raises his eyebrows. Rising, he reaches out to touch the end of my hair.

"Well?" I ask. My nerves pick up as I wait for his verdict. My body itches to pace, as I always do when nervous, but I force myself to stand still under his perusal.

"Amazing. You appear nothing like yourself."

*****

Rising early is my norm, so I'm up and repacked when Adrien is ready to go. The morning is sunny with the promise of being hot. Already the brightness of the desert sun distorts objects and makes me squint, even in sunglasses. On a short walk to a diner, we pass a few people, and cars travel down the street with the slight whiff of exhaust, but there's nothing suspicious in this small reservation community. The ceremonies will begin about midafternoon and continue into the night, so we have plenty of time to plan. We don't know when, or even if, we'll find what we're looking for, but at this point, the only direction is forward.

Sitting down to breakfast, we order blueberry pancakes for me and an omelet for Adrien.

I'm staring at Adrien, but can't seem to help it—he looks so different. When he came out of the bathroom the night before, I was shocked. His hair is now a dark, sandy blond and he's clean-shaven. A handsome face hid behind that trim beard.

"So, what's our plan?" I ask him between mouthfuls of sweet, fluffy pancakes.

""I have a contact who will ease our time at the village. I don't know if there will be any other observers, but let's hope so. The more visitors, the easier we will blend in. This time of year, there are many ceremonial dances occurring so seeing a few should be easy. Keep on the lookout for a kachina with the swastika symbol." After a sip of coffee, he continues. "We'll meet Kaya Mase within the hour. She'll get us into the village, and with her alongside us, we'll be able to stay and see the rites. While we are there, we should be safe from any outside influences that look to do us harm. We need to stay alert, find the kachina with the swastika, and finish our work there."

"Who's Kaya Mase?"

"I met some of the tribe years ago while researching the use of the swastika in different societies. She was very helpful and we became friends."

I nod my understanding but think, *foolproof, right*? My sense is, the fickle hand of fate is going to play a large part in the success or failure of this undertaking.

*****

An hour into our drive, Adrien turns onto a side street with a green sign that says OLD ORAIBI with an arrow. *Looks like we're here.* With a deep breath, I prepare myself.

The beauty of the Arizona vista is stunning. The landscape is bare and exposed, stripped of foliage other than cactus and a few scrub trees. One would think it'd be ugly and unappealing to the eye, but the reverse is true. The wind-swept mesas and brave plant life call to my soul in a very profound way. I see why the Hopi think they are at the center of the world.

Adrien parks the Honda, and we wait only a moment before a few young men arrive to look us over. Soon after, an attractive, middle-aged woman steps through the wall they've created. She's dressed in a traditional Hopi dress: it bares one shoulder, reaches her ankles, and is a beautiful green fabric. She has multiple beaded necklaces around her throat. Peeking from under her skirt are moccasins that look soft and comfortable. Her dark hair is shot through with gray and must be quite long because it's wound in two large buns, which remind me of Princess Leia of Star Wars fame.

When he sees her, Adrien steps from the car, and she comes eagerly forward to greet him with a hug.

"Adrien. It's good to see you."

"Kaya," he says with a gentle tone. "You are as beautiful as ever."

With a small blush, she reaches to touch his cheek. "Still the charmer. And who is this?" she asks, indicating me as I step from the car.

Adrien places his hand on her waist and leads her to me. "This is my friend Ellen. She is the one we spoke about. We need to observe some of the rites, Kaya. We seek a kachina, a specific kachina."

Kaya's eyes open wide and she doesn't seem to realizes she's wringing her hands. She peers at me. "What will happen if you find what you seek?"

"We don't know, Kaya," Adrien answers. "We only know we must try."

*****

Kaya, Adrien, and I wander with various groups of people who stop and watch dances as they occur. There's a hush of anticipation that precedes each as the kachina dancers climb from stone rooms dug into the earth. In each subterranean room, or *kiva,* there's a ladder designed to look authentic and ancient. As the dancers rise from the ground, it's as if we've stepped back in time. The costumes are beautiful with bright colors and varied ornaments; among them are feathers, silver, and fur. Many of the kachina dancers have large, artificial heads on their costumes and paint on their bodies. The masks are many times the size of a normal head, and Adrien explains that when wearing the mask, the dancer is believed to become the kachina the mask represents. Some clearly represent animals; others, spirits. In addition to fur and feathers, they have horns and snouts mounted on wood or leather.

As the day progresses, I am more and more privileged to bear witness to the ceremonies. Being here, among the Hopi, is not where I thought I'd ever be and I understand the opportunity afforded me.

"How do you know so much about the Hopi and their ceremonies?" I ask Adrien when there's a break in the dance.

With an eye on Kaya as she moves toward us, he

answers softly, "While studying the swastika and its use in different civilizations, I had the opportunity to spend time with the Hopi people. I learned many things."

I watch him with a tilt of my head, aware of his interest in Kaya. Questions rattle around in my mind, but there isn't time.

Another dance begins. The men in costume move together with small side steps as the drums beat and people chant. Out of the corner of my eye, I catch sight of a kachina watching us — watching me. When I turn my head to look directly at him, he's gone. Scanning left and right, trying to catch a glimpse of him, I swear I've seen this same figure other times today, but whenever I look, he's gone. Have I imagined him? I don't think he's a hallucination. It's definitely hot out, but we've continued to drink water and ate earlier after buying *piki*, a traditional bread, from an old woman. I feel fine. Maybe I should mention this figure to Adrien. I decide to wait and watch. I'll tell him if I see him again.

The sun flares a moment as it begins its decent below the red mesas, then disappears quickly. Torches are lit and the dances continue, though now they take on a different quality. The men truly seem to be spirits as they move in and out of the flickering light. With the addition of the torches, smoke fills the air. Tendrils of vapor float before us and partially obscure the ceremony. It makes me feel isolated. I'm aware of a sense of apprehension singing in my bones and I glance toward Adrien. He is spellbound by the dancers, and though he's close enough to touch, he seems a world apart. Kaya is not to be seen. The chanting is faint now.

Within the blink of an eye, everything changes. The

dancers, everything, everyone is in slow motion. The sounds are muted and my head feels bloated and dizzy, my eyelids heavy. Even my breathing is slow and labored, but loud in my head—the sound of it drowns out all others. The back of my mind is aware enough to question why I don't feel concern, but I shrug the questions off. My body is relaxed, my muscles loose. Every nuance of the costumes and the scene are in fine detail. The dancers stomp and the fringes and furs on them move slowly, the dirt creating small puffs at their feet. The burning cinders swirl and wisps of smoke float in the air. All sounds are hollow and distant.

My eyes are barely open. I'm groggy and my head's in a fog, but there's a slight buzz occurring. Since I was little, this feeling—this buzz—has preceded eventful happenings. If I weren't so foggy, I'd be more aware, concerned—observant. Captivated by the dancers, I'm hypnotized by their movements.

With a quick blink to focus, awareness creeps in that the kachina I've felt watching is here. He's on the other side of the dancers. His body is partially obscured by the mass of the crowd, but in the haze and blur of everything, he stands out clearly. He's perfectly still. His body is painted and his mask is large, with a snout and feathers. In his hand he holds a rattle, and on the rattle is a swastika.

My feet are immobile but my body sways with the subdued rhythm of the drums and the chants of the kachina dancers. I stare at the mystery kachina—*my* kachina—and he stares back. After what seems an eternity, he turns and walks away. Teetering forward, I want to yell to him but am unable to speak. My heart jumps in my chest when he turns back, and although he's in a mask, his gaze burns into me. Pivoting

34

again, he takes a step, stops, and looks my direction. *I get it. Follow me.* My body frees from its paralysis and I easily pass through the crowd of dancers and watchers. The world around us is like a slow-motion movie, but the kachina and I move at a natural speed. He walks away. As he moves into the night, I follow.

We pass through the village, through arcs of light thrown by torches. Following him, it's as if we're in a dream, an illusion. My brain refuses to concentrate on anything but him. He passes through light, where his costume shines brightly, and then into the dim darkness where only his outline is discernable. Light, dark, light, dark...

My legs ache and my lungs are winded by the time we approach the outskirts of another abandoned village. Amid the adobe buildings, in a central location is a kiva. It's dark, and only by the light of the moon is the boulder-lined, subterranean hole visible. It has a ladder extending from its edge. The kachina grasps the ladder, swings a leg over and descends. He doesn't look back. Hesitating at the top of the kiva for a moment, I tell myself I'm not sure I should go down. I'll be putting myself at risk. But really, there's no question. Of course I'll go into the hole. Of course I'll follow him to see what can be learned.

With a hand on the ladder, I throw a leg over to start down. It gets darker the lower I go into the hole — rung by rung. The deeper I go, the cooler the air feels against my skin, and there's the scent of old smoke and dirt. Under my hands, the ladder is smooth and worn with use and time. I continue down, moving step to step. The ladder's slightly darker silhouette is barely visible under my hands. With a final stretch, my foot hits the floor, and I've reached the bottom. I step from the ladder, but keep one hand on it. It's my only orientation in the room other than the slightly lighter hole above. Tipping my head back, I stare at the sky. It's beautiful, mesmerizing. The stars shine, and my eyes follow one as it shoots across the night.

Somehow, I'm overcome with a sense of peace. With a deep breath, I peer into the darkness of the kiva.

"Hello?" I raise my voice. *Is the kachina still here or am I alone?*

Without warning, there's an intense flare of light that causes me to jump back, almost tripping on the edge of the ladder. I shut my eyes tight and cover them with my arm. The brightness blinds me for a moment and disorients me. Blinking rapidly, I cautiously open my eyes to see a fire burning in a central pit. The room is circular, constructed with rough stone. The walls have spaces, which look as if they might have been used as sleeping platforms.

The kachina stands a few feet in front of me.

He drifts slowly toward me. His footsteps are completely silent on the dirt floor. With a deep breath, I stand my ground, though my eyes get bigger and bigger and my head tips back on my neck the closer he gets. When he's within a foot of me, he reaches out and my medallion lifts from my skin. Mesmerized, I watch it hover, bobbing gently toward his reach, but there's no strain on my neck. My breath comes in bursts as I look at my medallion floating. Is he magnetic? How's this happening? Slowly, my eyes move from my medallion to the face of the kachina. Peering into his eyes, I feel a bolt of lightning hit my body, and my brain shorts out as everything goes black.

*****

The wheel spins; the players awaken.
Not thought, not sight–only heart will find what you seek.
And so, it begins…

"Ellen, Ellen wake up."

Adrien's voice is far away. Everything is dark and calm; I want to stay here forever.

"Ellen!" His voice is louder, stricter, but shaking with worry. "Please step back. Give her some air! Can someone get some water?"

Coming back now, I feel him grab my shoulder and give me a shake. *Oh, Adrien. Leave me be. This place is nice.*

"Ellen! Are you all right? Wake up!" And then lower, he whispers, "Ellen, please. You must be all right."

With a tremendous effort, my awareness pushes to the front of my consciousness, and slowly I open my eyes. With a blink, Adrien comes into focus. Past him, a throng of people watch us.

Apparently, I've become the show.

Adrien's shoulders slump as his breath leaves his frame. A smile creases his face. "There you are, my dear. Are you all right? You dropped over without warning."

With a wrinkle of my brow, I look to the crowd of people. My mind spins with a million questions. I wrench my head left and right and note we're on the hard-packed ground where the dances take place. The last thing in my memory is being in the kiva, the kachina making my medallion float…then nothing. The beginnings of a throbbing headache pulse in my temples, and thinking is difficult.

I touch my medallion. It's as always—warm with the heat of my skin, a solid weight.

"What is it, Ellen?" Adrien watches me closely.

With my other hand, I reach to touch him, to prove he's real. Arm outstretched, almost at his face, I notice my hand is closed in a loose fist. Still fuzzy and in a fog, I tilt my hand to open my grip. Lying on my palm is a beautiful, delicately etched, heart-shaped leaf. It's shining golden in the firelight. With a gasp of shock, I sit up, catching myself on my other arm. My head swims and my vision blurs. Again, the words come clearly to my mind:

The wheel spins; the players awaken.
Not thought, not sight — only heart will find what you seek.
And so, it begins…

Blinking rapidly, I shake my head to clear it and make sense of everything that is happening. There is no memory about this leaf. Tentatively, I touch it with my finger and turn it over. It's thin and fragile. Inscribed on the back is a string of symbols I can't decipher.

乐山大佛

With bewilderment, I glance at Adrien. He has a stunned look on his face as if he's taken a hit to the head. In a hushed whisper, he says, "The Buddha."

I wrinkle my brow and shake my head again. Obviously, he knows more than he's told me. We really need to talk.

Chapter 5

Adrien and I sit in the Honda a few miles out of Tuba City. We're in the middle of nowhere and there's no one around but us. It's night, but even now, the beauty of the desert takes my breath away. Silhouettes of mesas break the horizon in the distance and cacti throw shadows cast by the moonlight. A coyote calls and a tingle runs down my spine, causing a small shiver. These sensations pull at me. I love the nights, the feel and the scent of the darkness. In me is an urge to jump from the car and run—just run like a night animal, for the sheer pleasure of it.

Adrien's talking, explaining what happened at the village. His voice pulls my mind from its reverie and my gaze from the landscape.

"You're telling me I never left the ceremonial area? I was there with you all along, watching the dancers, until suddenly fainting?" There's skepticism in my tone and I don't even try to hide it. My disbelief is obvious. "Maybe you were affected by the smoke. It didn't seem like only wood was burning in those torches."

"Ellen, the Hopi are deeply spiritual people."

"And?" With a scowl, I throw up my hands and shake my head at him.

"Perhaps what you experienced was a Spirit Walk."

"*What?*" A chuckle escapes my lips. "Do you really think the most probable of all possibilities is my spirit left my body and walked through the night with a kachina?" I choke on a laugh.

Adrien sits, his face stern, his expression unwavering. He's crazy and I'm stressed.

"I'm sorry, Adrien. Men broke into my house, so I know *something* is going on, but I don't believe I just 'walked with the spirits' or some other absurd thing. And what about the words?"

"What words?"

"The words. The words, like a song in my head. Didn't you hear them?" The question has a shrill quality, even to my ears. The idea of words that aren't mine reverberating in my head is terrifying.

"There weren't any words, Ellen. Tell me what you heard. Perhaps we can make sense of it."

I repeat the lines to him. "The wheel spins, the players awaken. Not thought, not sight—only heart will find what you seek. And so, it begins..."

"Hmm..." With a long look out the windshield into the distance, Adrien rubs his fingers over his newly shorn chin. The rasping of stubble seems harsh to my ears in the quiet of the car. "This obviously has to do with the prophecy. The wheel spinning—it's a reference to the medallion and the swastika. Many civilizations regard the swastika as a spinning wheel, or a representation of the sun. It's beginning, and we're on the right path." He looks at me with a large, pleased grin on his face. "They're speaking to you, Ellen. You see? You *are* the Key."

His words fill me with disquiet. What if I don't want to be the Key? What if I want to go home and continue my peaceful life? I don't want to be part of this. All I can do is stare at him. He visibly hums with excitement.

Almost to himself, he asks, "But the second line. What could that mean? Not thought, not sight—only heart will find what you seek. Not thought. Not sight. Only heart."

"Adrien, there's been a mistake. I'm sure I'm not the person to figure this out." My temperature rises the more we talk about this. It's as if a ton of weight sits on my chest, and with a shaking hand, I wipe a line of sweat from my upper lip.

He watches me closely, his brows drawn together. "What are you talking about? You heard the words. They were spoken only to you." He leans toward me, placing his elbow on the center console. "And how do you explain your experience with the kachina? You yourself said one moment you were in the kiva and the next you were lying on the ground."

41

"Right. The electrical jolt knocked me out, and when I came to, I was with you." This explanation sounds completely logical. Can't I just forget everything and go home?

But he continues to push at me.

With narrowed eyes, he asks, "Did the kachina carry you back? I didn't see you leave and I certainly didn't see you come back in the arms of a kachina. How do you explain coming and going and the fact your body didn't move?" He shifts in his seat slightly toward me and lays his hand on my arm. "Ellen, you know after your experiences in Europe last year you are, how should I say this...intuitive." Adrien gazes at me with that intense look and truth be told, I don't like it very much. "If you think back, you will agree you've always been able to read situations. You've known where to find an object or how to answer a probing question."

What he says is true, but he doesn't even know the half of it. When younger, I thought everyone knew certain things; things like where my mother left the broach she got from her grandmother. Everyone figured it was lost, but I knew it had slipped down between the bed and the wall. As I aged, a vibration or buzz began. It started at the top of my head and would precede these situations. My parents accepted these feelings as part of me, without question. Little did I know, they thought I was something more than I am. As I grew, I came to realize not everyone sensed things this way. I learned to keep the information to myself. It only took a few weird looks in grade school to understand being different wasn't something I desired. Last year, this ability became useful in my search for a lost piece of artwork. The more I opened myself to it, the easier and stronger it became.

"How do you know this? Did my parents discuss me

with you? And besides," I say, blowing him off with a wave of my hand, "sensing where lost items are is different than seeing and receiving an item from a ghost."

He gives a small shrug. "Maybe, maybe not. We did discuss you, Ellen. They worried for you."

"There was never any indication they were worried about me. It was all innocent; no danger was involved."

Adrien releases my hand and in an obvious attempt to change the subject, says, "It's plain you need some time to come to terms with what this will all mean to you and where we will take it. Let's back up and give you some distance. You look to be ready to bolt."

He's right. Leaning toward the door, I've grabbed the handle as if planning to fling it open.

"About the kachina and the words—for now, why don't we agree that something happened. The result is the leaf."

There are questions, so many questions. Concerns about the kachina and the words. But, for now, I'm willing to shelve the discussion to give me time to think about everything he's told me. Sitting straight in the car seat, I pull myself away from the door where I'd been crouching, ready to flee. "Fine. Let's change the subject, for now, and leave the matter of the kachina and the words open. We'll agree that we disagree with what happened, but we do have the leaf. So, talk to me. What did you mean 'the Buddha?'"

"Please, Ellen. May I see the leaf again?"

After reaching back between the seats to unzip my bag, I pull a small wooden box out and set it on my lap. With a deep breath, I open the latch.

We look at the leaf lying in the box. The wooden box was brought on a whim, and now I'm glad. It's small enough to contain some items tightly so they don't get banged up, and big enough to be useful. Its original purpose must have been a jewelry box, since the inside is lined with a red, velvety fabric. It's the perfect spot to place the leaf.

Leery and uncertain, almost afraid to touch it, I hand the entire box to Adrien. Before he accepts it, he reaches and turns on the overhead lights. My eyes squint as they adjust; I'd grown accustomed to the dark.

Within the illumination of the front seat, Adrien takes the box and sets it on his lap. There the leaf sits, and we watch it like a living entity, waiting for it to do something, anything to explain what it is and how it came to be in my hand.

My attention is pulled from the leaf toward Adrien as he speaks.

"Gautama Buddha, or simply 'Buddha — The Enlightened One,' is represented by four symbols."

I gaze at him, instantly captivated by the topic and information.

"They are the *stupa*, the *Dharma wheel*, the *lotus flower*, and the *Bodhi tree*. The *stupa* is a place of meditation, which contains the remains of monks and other relics; the *Dharma wheel* represents the path of the Buddha's teaching; the *lotus flower* represents enlightenment above the mud of our human lives; and the fourth, the *Bodhi tree,* is said to be the tree under which the Buddha achieved enlightenment. A representation of the *Bodhi tree* is often its leaves. They are a distinctive heart shape. It's that leaf you had in your hand after your Spirit Walk. The leaf we see here."

At the term Spirit Walk, I give him a sharp look. Apparently, he isn't letting that argument go. Dropping my gaze from him, I look to the leaf. It's beautiful. Fragile. A thin, delicate metal finely detailed with realistic venation.

I lean toward him, peering along his shoulder to see the leaf from a different angle. "Okay. I get you think this represents a leaf from a *Bodhi tree,* but maybe it's not. What I see is a beautiful piece of artwork that could be almost any type of leaf from a thousand different trees."

"What you are forgetting is the etching on the reverse side." Saying this, he gently turns the leaf over. Once again, the inscription is visible.

乐山大佛

"What does it mean? And how does this relate to the swastika symbol?" Closer, I lean forward and across the seats in anticipation of more information.

"The mountain is a Buddha, and a Buddha is a mountain."

Watching him, I wait for him to say something else. To clarify the subject in some way. What did he mean?

"Ok…um…could you be more cryptic?"

He breaks into a huge smile. "In Chinese, the etching on the back means, basically, Leshan Giant Buddha."

"Leshan Giant Buddha?" I repeat with a raise of my eyebrows.

"Yes. Buddha. The swastika is a symbol of Buddhism. It is 'the heart of Buddha' and is etched on many Buddha sculptures mid-chest."

"How do you know this?"

"I know many things about many things," he says with a twinkle in his eye.

A smile comes to my face. "Weird. How can the swastika represent so many things to so many different people?"

"That's the mystery, isn't it?"

"So, does this mean we're going to China?"

He nods at me. "There are over a million Buddhists in China and many, many Buddha. Luckily, we know which Buddha we're looking for."

"The Leshan Giant Buddha?"

"Yes, my dear. Yes, indeed."

"How will we get to China? How will we do it without attracting attention?"

"Leave that to me." He has a huge smile on his face and seems extremely pleased. My smile widens as I look back at him. My terror is fleeing in the face of this adventure. I don't have any idea what we're doing or what the result will be, but apparently, we know our next stop.

Chapter 6

The city appears out the window of our jet. Night slowly descends, running its inky black fingers over and between the buildings, forcing out the light of day. The panorama is spellbinding as the city rises from Kowloon Bay as if it sprang full grown. There are skyscrapers with colors and lights. Magnificent lights like a hundred million fireflies twinkling in the darkness. As we pass over Hong Kong toward our destination, the Chek Lap Kok Airport — or Hong Kong International — I watch. The airport is located on an island just west of the city. Adrien and I will locate transportation into Hong Kong and then inland to Leshan. I can say with certainty, I never thought I'd gaze down at Hong Kong from an airplane. The city is huge. It's nearly a "megacity," with a little over seven million people in its borders.

*****

Before we left Phoenix, Adrien made a quick stop to purchase a prepaid cell. We took photos of each other, which he sent…somewhere. When asked, he gave me that inscrutable stare and said nothing. Soon after, he made a stop at a US post office. He double-parked the Honda, which I mentioned wasn't the smartest, and while I waited, he ran in and soon ran out. He climbed into the car, tossed a small packet onto my lap, and drove away.

"What's this?" I asked hesitantly.

"Open it."

Picking at the tape with my fingernail for a moment, I got the packet open. With a shake, the upended contents spilled onto my lap. Silently and disbelievingly, I stared at them. "Papers," nefarious characters call them, I believe. False documents. False documents with Adrien's and my face on them.

I didn't want to touch them. Adrien calmly and steadily drove toward the airport.

"Who in the hell are you? You tell me you have contacts, but who are you really?" I asked quietly, watching him, attempting to see some crack in the shell surrounding a man I once thought I knew. His eyes glanced from the road to my face to the papers on my lap and back to the road, but he didn't speak.

"Is your name even Adrien?"

"Ellen..." he began, but then stopped. Again, his eyes did the tri-jump from me to papers to road. "All I ask is for you to give me your trust. Have conviction in our quest."

Conviction. A firm belief. Such a funny concept, to believe without proof. If I don't at least attempt to have confidence in this man and this situation, I might as well throw in the towel, head home, and let come what may.

So, I trusted him, and with aliases in place, Jacques Louis and Linda Nelson boarded a plane for Hong Kong, China. They sat separately. They didn't talk or even look at each other. To even the most observant eye, they appeared as strangers traveling to a foreign land; strangers who just happened to be on the same flight.

*****

The twenty hours of flight are exhausting, but much of the time is spent doing my homework. Leshan and the Giant Buddha are major tourist attractions, so we'll be able to make our way there easily. They can be reached from Hong Kong by trolley, bus, or private car. Each option consists of crossing from the separately-governed Hong Kong—a Special Administrative Region—to Shenzhen on the mainland, which means we'll need to go through two sets of customs. The most expensive option, but the one with the least hassle and time, will be the private car. After landing, but prior to gathering our belongings, Adrien and I have a quick discussion, and he agrees this is our best option.

Baggage in hand, we head via shuttle to a nearby hotel. We need a clean place to sleep. Tomorrow we'll be entering mainland China, so we choose a hotel close to the airport. At this point, Adrien and I have shared so many rooms, it would feel funny to have a space of my own. One nice thing this affords, however, is the ability to discuss our situation privately.

"Tell me more about the poem."

"Minds far greater than mine consider it a prophecy. A foretelling of things that will be, that must be."

Sitting silently, I wait for more, my mind replaying the lines of the poem—prophecy. "Now that I remember it, the beat and the words won't leave my head. They're bouncing around in there, making me wanna go nuts trying to understand it."

Nodding his head in agreement, Adrien says, "I appreciate that, but many more people than you and I have tried to decipher the prophecy, all to no avail."

Okay. I want to gnash my teeth with frustration when it's apparent the information is going to have to be pulled out of him. "So? Did they discover anything? Why am I in the middle of this?"

Adrien stares at me for a moment. Breaking eye contact, he looks off into a corner of the room, and his focus seems to turn inward. "Based on the wording of the prophecy, there are beings we are watched by. Are they good? Are they evil? Perhaps they are a little of both. It does not appear they can influence man, but simply exist to...I do not know...monitor? Their purpose is unclear, but knowledge of these beings is in our lore, our stories. The desire to know more is driven by good people like your parents and bad people like the men at your home—the Guild.

"What if there were a way to converse with one or more

of the Guardians? How might we help the peoples of the world? Or, I am sure the question has been asked, how powerful could a man be if he were in control of a Guardian? No one knows their location. Are they real or imagined? Based on the words you heard in the village, it would appear the Guardians are quite real. What the function of the Key is, we have no idea, other than to locate the new Guardian." He gives a little shrug, his focus still lost in his thoughts.

"Well, hell. Do they know *anything*? How are we supposed to work with all the blank spaces?" I jump up to pace in the small room.

From his seat, Adrien draws in his feet to give me more area and to protect his extremities from being stomped on as I stride by.

"So, a new cycle is starting? And what is this cycle? Somehow the Key is integral in finding this new 'Guardian?'" I say, making quote marks in the air.

Adrien turns and watches me pace. "Yes. Yes, it would appear to be so. We don't truly understand what the cycle is. We simply follow the prophecy and wait for the Key."

"And you're thinking I'm this Key," I say, poking my chest with my own finger. "Though we don't know what that means. We need to figure out my part in all of this. The very idea of being in the middle of something I don't understand is terrifying for me. Why me? What do I need to do?"

"My belief is in being the Key, you must find the answer to the clue you were given. It will lead you forward." Adrien, always so patient and scholarly. He looks at me with wide eyes that encourage me to ask my questions, run through scenarios.

"Forward to where? And the words, the words from the

village—you think they're a clue. A clue to where we're to go? Information we're to learn, or what?"

"Yes, Ellen. That is why you, and only you, could hear the words." He nods at me.

Throwing my hands in the air, I whisper, "But why me, Adrien? Why me?"

"You were too young to remember when your mother first came by the medallion you wear. She was in a small town near Taos, New Mexico. She said afterward, she was...how did she put it? Oh, yes, inspired! She was inspired to go shopping." Adrien gives a small, sad smile and shakes his head gently. "Your father and I laughed at that. Your mother never needed a reason to go shopping. She had you with her and had only a short drive from their current home to this village. I do not even remember its name.

"As she stated it, she was walking with you, and suddenly you veered off, shooting toward a shop like a rocket. She yelled your name and headed after you, sweeping you up in her arms to keep you from touching any of the merchandise. She was astounded when you threw a fit, arching your body, kicking your feet, making a racket. You were always such a good child; she didn't know what to do, and so she set you back down. You immediately headed for a display and grabbed an item. You refused to release it, and your mother felt she had to purchase it or she would be dealing with World War III right there in that little shop, in that little town."

At the end of his story, I sit down heavily beside him, my body weak. "My medallion?"

"Yes. How it had gotten there and how long it had been there is anyone's guess. Of course, your mother recognized the medallion for what it was. We all know what it looks like—in a general sense, at least. The medallion, and your reaction, scared her though. It wasn't until years later she was comfortable enough with the path it would take you on that she gifted it back to you." Adrien stops and is quiet for a few moments before looking up and again catching my eye. "So, you ask, 'Why you?' I guess you'd know the reason to that better than anyone else."

*****

The next day, we're swept through customs by our highly efficient driver. He's very personable and understands most things we say, though his English is limited. He introduces himself simply as Kang and seems very sincere in his attempts to make our trip enjoyable. We're not even required to get out of our car; he handles everything. In Shenzhen, Kang takes us directly to the airport, where we have a limited wait until we board a plane to Yibin. The flight is uneventful, and takes a little under two hours. The city of Yibin is covered in a cloud of smog which impedes our view of the area. It reminds me of larger cities in America.

In Yibin, we catch a car that takes us to Leshan. The countryside is beautiful—lush and green. There are densely packed trees, waterways, and hills that poke out as if they were placed there as an afterthought. In Leshan, we look for a quick, inexpensive hotel, and after we inform our driver of our wishes, he takes us to the Leshan Golden Leaf Express. Staying here, we'll be within two and a half miles of the Giant Buddha. I want to head to the Buddha right away, but Adrien prevails on me to wait until tomorrow. He wants to check the area and be prepared for any eventualities that may occur.

At night, I dream of symbols, family, and random lines from the prophecy and the words from the Hopi village. They flash through my mind without end, over and over like a broken movie reel. The faces of my mother and father swim in a sea of swastikas, Buddha, kachina, and many others I don't recognize.

In the morning, I rouse before my alarm, eyes open. Adrien's steady breathing comes from the next bed, and I'm comforted by his presence. My mind is wide awake but not rested. My body lies on sheets, twisted and covered in old sweat, and my pajamas are stuck to my skin. I'm unable to recall my entire dream, but it felt as if it went on for hours. I can still hear the echo of my mother's voice. *Acceptance. Faith.*

*****

The next morning, we catch a bus crowded with people. Soon we're at the area around the Giant Buddha. There are many people coming and going; it's obviously a popular tourist attraction. Most of the people are Asian, but there are Western dialects, also. So many different looks, ages, and types of people. Adrien's is the only French accent I'm able to perceive and I'm the only American. As tall as I am, I can look over Adrien's head, which puts me far taller than the locals. Aware of people watching me, both covertly and openly, I try to ignore them. Some give me funny looks. Even in America, I'm taller than the norm at five-foot-eight. Have they ever seen a woman my height?

We're told there are different ways to view the Giant Buddha, but one of the most popular is by ferry boat. Deciding this will give us the best overall perspective, we wait in line to board one of the many ferries as I try to ignore the heavy smell of fish and river water in the air. My attention is diverted as Adrien fills me in on the history of the Giant Buddha.

"The Leshan Giant Buddha sits at the juncture of the Minjiang, Dadu, and Qingyi rivers. Construction began in 713 by a Chinese monk named Hai Tong. Because the three rivers come together at that spot, the shipping vessels traveling up and down the river were in danger from the turbulent waters. The locals believed a spirit who lived there caused the waters to be hazardous. Hai Tong had faith that the building of a Buddha would calm the spirit and make water travel safe for the boats."

Listening to Adrien and watching the people around us are not keeping my thoughts silent. Constantly, in the back of my mind, is the line from the village, the line I can't understand: not thought, not sight — only heart will find what you seek. I continue to bang up against it. Will I ever understand?

Adrien continues with his lesson in the history of the Giant Buddha. "Unfortunately, Hai Tong died before seeing the construction complete, and seventy years later, a *jiedushi* or regional commander sponsored the completion of the project, which was finished in 803. In an amazing turn of events, the displacement of rock and dirt during the construction was deposited into the rivers and did indeed alter their flow, which made them safe for boat travel."

I smile to myself at this information. One could say, "Buddha works in mysterious ways."

When our turn in line comes, Adrien pays our toll and we board the ferry for the trip past the Buddha. We'll pass within twenty or thirty feet of the cliff face. While living in Detroit I had the opportunity to be on the water, but when I moved to Phoenix, I had yet to make the time to visit any of the lakes in the surrounding areas. Stepping from the dock to the moving deck of the ferry, I'm happy to realize I still have my sea legs. The brown water of the rivers moves rapidly. There are quite a few boats currently on the water, and the weather is a little windy and chilly. I'm glad to have my jacket.

As we near the location of the Buddha, my eyes run up the towering length of a staircase cut from the side of the mountain. People, packed on the stairs, move upward at a slow but steady pace. All around, red rock, lush, dark green vegetation, and trees cover the mountain. With the addition of people and the colors they wear, it's an amazing visual.

Adrien stands next to me at the rail, and anticipation streams off him. There's almost a scent to his nerves, and it makes me edgy. I reach forward and grab the metal rail, holding on tight as we round the bend in the river and the Buddha comes into sight.

"Wow..." My breath leaves my lungs in a rush. The crowd on the boat makes a tipping motion forward as if they're made of iron and the Buddha is a magnet. Looking up and up, I crane my head back on my neck. It's hard to describe the immensity of it and how small and insignificant it makes us seem. The Buddha sits on a cliff face that is about twenty feet tall depending on the depth of the river, and from there he rises 223 feet. He was carved sitting with his hands resting on his legs. His bare feet stick out from his garments and they're almost as tall as a man; five or so people could sit on a toe nail. Tourists encircle the front of the Buddha. They move like a swarm of insects to the other side to begin the climb up a set of stairs that mirrors the one we saw coming in. There are hundreds of people on or near him. As they climb the stairs, they pass near his head and ear on his right side.

"We'll have to go inland and get a closer look." I lean toward Adrien as I speak. Unable to rip my gaze from the Buddha's face, my voice comes out a whisper, as if I've entered a church. The statue is magnificent. His hair is fashioned in hundreds of small coils and his eyes are slightly squinted.

We're traveling along in front of the cliff when out of the side of my vision I see—or sense, really—an object afloat in the water next to the cliff face. It disappears as the waves move, then appears again. It's...it can't be. It looks like...

A lotus?

"Adrien, do you see the lotus next to the cliff?"

"What?" Adrien looks at me as if his attention had to be physically pulled.

He scans the area of the Buddha, searching left and right.

"No, Adrien." I point, peering down the length of my arm. "Down at the water's edge."

"What, Ellen? I don't see anything."

The lotus floats happily in the water. Can't he see it? It's as plain as day; in fact, it has a slight glow.

"You did say a lotus? Where do you see it?"

Adrien swings his head left and right again and pushes to his toes next to the railing. He's a bit frantic in his attempt to locate the flower.

"It's okay, Adrien," I say and pat his arm gently. I get it

now. It came in a rush. Why didn't I understand before? The answer was right in front of me. Leaving my hand on his shoulder and shifting my weight, I pick up one foot to pull off a boot. Then, I reverse my stance and pull off the other boot.

"What are you doing?" He stares intently at me.

I break the contact and lean over to pick up the boots.

"Don't lose these; they're my favorites and it took me forever to break them in."

When I hand the boots to him, he automatically takes them into his arms.

"Ellen..."

With a quick motion, I unzip and remove my jacket and hand it to him, too. He takes it gingerly. He looks me up and down and just as he moves forward as if to stop me, I stop him with a quick touch on his shoulder.

"Faith, Adrien. Not thought or sight, just heart. It's a leap of faith," I say, putting my hand on the rail to vault over the side.

As I hit the water, a gasp explodes from my lips. It's cold. Really cold. While treading water, I push my hair out of my face with one hand and glance back and up at the boat. The people behind me, on the ferry, rush to the edge of the deck. They all babble in amazement. I'm pretty amazed myself. Amid the local folk, I locate Adrien. His eyes are enormous in his pale face and he has a death grip on my belongings. I spin back toward the cliff face and swim. I'm a pretty good swimmer and not that far out, but the pull of the river makes it extremely tiring. As the water crests, pushing me higher, the lotus comes into sight and then I lose it again when my body drops into a swell. It's clear what direction I'm going, though—there's a 223-foot Buddha towering over me to guide my way. As I near the cliff, faces of tourists pop over the edge to watch me. Between the people on the ferries and the people at the Buddha, I have quite the audience.

The river water has zero visibility. It's muddy brown and has an unpleasant smell—like sludge and fish. The exertion of swimming isn't warming me, and my fingers and feet are going numb. My breath comes in little gasps; this is nothing like swimming laps in an indoor pool.

In a few more moments, the lotus is near. Its presence leaves me torn: glad it's still there and wishing it weren't. If it were my imagination, I could be pulled on board, warmed, and maybe go home.

This close, the lotus is exquisite. It's larger than it should be, pearly in color, and as before, it emits a gentle glow. As I maneuver within arm's reach, it drops below the surface of the water as if pulled by a string.

"What the…?" I mutter softly, spinning to look frantically around.

Moving to where the lotus was, a soft illumination glitters under the surface. It's murky in the brown gunk and though the flower isn't visible, I'm sure it's creating the light. Uncertain, I glance at the ferry. It's quite far away now. Treading water, I look down at the light. With a deep breath, I dive after the flower.

As I push my body deeper into the river, the light of the lotus stays ahead of me. We continue to move downward. Uncertain how far I've swam, the need to breathe grows more incessant. I'm becoming more certain I should go back when our angle changes to a cross-ward trajectory. With bursts of adrenaline pulsing through my system, there's an awakening perception of panic—at this point, panic will be deadly. With a hard kick to pick up my speed, my lungs begin to seriously protest. A bubble escapes my mouth, and my strokes become more thrashing than swimming when suddenly the light from the lotus disappears. In bewilderment, I halt all forward motion, hanging in the water, waiting for it to reappear. It's cold and black. I'm all alone and harbor a certain knowledge my death is near. At this point, losing any guide, I don't know which way is forward. Another bubble forces its way out of my mouth as my lungs contract, greedy for oxygen, and drowning becomes a real possibility. A surge of animalistic terror overcomes me, and I push toward the surface, but in two short kicks, I rack my head on stone.

It's a cave!

I'm buried!

If I could scream, I would. My scream would reverberate until my world turned inside out and I could never speak again. Banging against the ceiling in some vain struggle to get through, I scratch at the stone to somehow find air. Distantly, there's the sensation of warmth on my head, but it doesn't register, that or the pain in my hands and fingers. Right at the last moment, the moment when there will be no choice but to suck the river into my lungs, a faded light pierces the water. Angling toward it like a hound after a scent in a jerky, frantic motion, I flail forward and gasp as my head breaks the surface of the water.

Lying more in the water than out, my head rests on a stone stair and my face basks in the cool air. There's no strength in me to move. My breath, harsh and raspy, echoes hollowly in the space. My throat burns as if I've swallowed acid, and every couple of gasps a coughing fit pushes my face back into the water. Blinking rapidly, I feel something sticky run into my eye, and I gingerly reach to touch it. With a blank look, I gape at the red, smearing it between my thumb and forefingers. I'm bleeding. Within me, there's a vague memory of cracking my head on the stone ceiling in the water tunnel. I can barely tell what blood is from my head and what flows from my hands and fingers, they are so torn up. There's a memory of ripping at the stone in an attempt to break through. Never have I felt panic like that. I felt like an animal, running on a gut reaction which had nothing to do with a thought or plan. I'm feeling doubly lucky to be alive while realizing how thoroughly I lost it.

Finally able to catch my breath, though my throat is going to hurt for days and my lungs feel torn apart, I lift my head. It spins and my vision fluctuates in and out. Concentrating hard, I stare at the stairs, which continue up and plateau. The lower ones are covered in a wet slime that has a repugnant smell, a smell I now share from lying upon them. Moving cautiously, I drag myself out of the water and up the stairs to peer across the floor.

At the far end is a Buddha—it appears to be an exact replica of the Giant Buddha, only in miniature. With a pivot of my head in the faded light, I study the room and note faint etchings on the walls and old sconces holding blackened torches. It's dim here and visibility is limited. The only illumination comes from a set of holes, one on each side, many feet up near the ceiling of the room. I think I'm inside the Giant Buddha.

Pulling myself to my feet, shivering in the cold air, I slowly walk toward the smaller statue. Though it's barely perceivable, the buzz is occurring in my head. There are so many sensations and pains happening in my body, I can't concentrate on them all. With an exhausted step, my feet drag along the floor, and the scrape of them echoes hollowly. If I stumble, I won't have the strength to get back up.

My gaze is caught by the Buddha. He's slightly taller than me in height and nearly three times as wide. There are old, dried flowers, puddles of wax that appear to be remnants of candles, and other crushed plants—herbs and possibly more flowers. These items surround the area where he sits. On his lap is a plate constructed of some silver metal, and on the plate is a gold item.

Should I touch anything? At this point, there's not much to lose. Approaching the Buddha, I step onto his platform. With a stretch, I reach out to pick up the object from the plate. At the last moment, I stop and pull my hand back, visions of Indiana Jones running through my head—maybe there is something to lose. Looking left and right, listening intently to discover any danger, I take a deep breath and hold it, analyzing the scents. Muddy water, dirt, a hint of old smoke, and cold. Even if I were to smell something unusual, I don't know what I'd do with the information. Luckily, everything seems perfectly normal considering I'm essentially buried inside a statue. I reach out again and gingerly retrieve the object. Pausing, focusing hard on my senses, I reach to hear or feel any change. Okay. No big boulder rolling out of anywhere to crush me...

Gazing down at the item, I shift the metallic square in my hand, feeling its hefty weight. It must be about two inches by two inches, and boldly imprinted on the front is a crude swastika. Turning it over, I note the same image appears on the reverse side, though in smaller detail, and other etchings surround it: swirls, what looks like a rudimentary alligator, and a couple of figures. I have no idea what it is or what it's used for, but I'm guessing it's what I'm after.

I close my fingers over the object in my hand, and my sight blanks. Words fill my head:

Like spokes of a wheel, the skills are set.
Truth and honesty are swept aside.
Search deep and triumph well...

My eyes blink slowly — once, twice. My fist, held out in front of me, fills my vision. How long have I been frozen in this position? It's getting darker; the sun is going down. The metal shard is in my hand, and the words reverberate in my head. I need to move. There's nothing to light the torches, if they'd even relight with the ancient material on the end. Other than the Buddha, torches, and the old offerings around the statue, there's nothing in this chamber. How am I going to get out? The thought of swimming back, while maybe possible, fills me with a sense of dread so profound my heart begins to beat a heavy rhythm in my chest, and my body breaks out in an icy sweat. Quickly, I wander around to look for any hint of an exit. Moving along the walls, I run my fingers over the symbols scratched into the stone. Even with the thought of escape on the forefront of my brain, my attention is captured by the etchings. There's a figure that looks like a number three, but it also has a circle shape next to it and lines above; symbols that resemble the swastika; a few that look like a beetle with long antennae attached to a handle-bar mustache; and among these are six-sided stars, crosses, and what appear to be yin and yang symbols. Astonishingly, all the religions of the world seem to be represented on these ancient walls.

So intent am I on the inscriptions that I'm startled as a mouse scurries past me, brushing my foot.

"Oh!" I say and jump back to the side, causing my shoulder to come in contact with the wall.

"Wait!" I yell with the realization I'm not alone. Surely this mouse didn't swim here. "Where did you go?" I ask aloud into the room as I swing left and right, hoping to catch sight of it again.

I slide the metal object into my front pants pocket and stoop to scour the floor in an attempt to startle the rodent into movement. As I continue down the side of the Buddha and toward his back, the mouse runs from a low crevice in the wall. It jumps past me and dashes up the back of the statue where it joins the wall and disappears about five feet up.

"What the hell?" I mutter, and without taking a moment to contemplate failure, I surge after. My stockinged feet are partially dried, and amazingly, they grip pretty well on the stone surface of the Buddha. The cuts on my hands are painful, but I don't care. If there's another way out of here, I'm on it. In the process of my Buddha climb, I slip a few times but continue until I'm standing precariously on his head and one shoulder. From here, vines spread on the walls, and the air is heavy with the scent of growing vegetation instead of dirt and water. I lean into the plants and finger my way through them, expecting to hit stone, but that doesn't happen. My hand disappears and then my arm with it. On my skin is the moist tickle of the vines' leaves. Are they trying to keep me here or help me escape? With a deep breath, I push my other arm, head, and upper body through the opening, kicking against the wall to force myself up and forward. Grabbing ahold of anything I can get my fingers around, I pull. The space is pitch black and cramped, and I utter a prayer of thanks that I'm long and lean. Inching my way forward, with only my sense of touch to guide me, my concentration is on keeping my mind blank except for the task at hand — grasp, pull, grasp, pull. While not claustrophobic in the general sense, this tunnel is pushing at all my instincts. I continue on and after a bit the tunnel narrows even further. Without warning, a burst of panic overwhelms me and the vision of my body trapped in this space is like a flashing light in my brain.

"Please, please, please..." I repeat this one word over and over like a mantra. Deep breath in, deep breath out. *Keep moving, Ellen. Slow and sure wins the race.*

I've been doing this for ages. With a belly crawl, I pull with my hands and scooch my toes to move myself forward against the friction of stone. Suddenly, my fingers dangle into open air, so I reach out, flailing with my hands to grasp something but there's nothing within reach. Bringing to bear my elbows and shoulders, inching forward, I wiggle my hips like a snake. When my head breaks into the surface of the cool night, I pause. My breath catches in a gasp and ready tears come to my eyes. Laying my head to the side, I inhale the night air with deep pulls from my chest. With a sob, I utter, "Thank you, thank you, thank you..." I take a moment for my sanity to return before I continue pulling myself forward. The slope of the hill is steep and as I emerge, I attempt to support myself but lose my grip. Birthed from the hillside, I slide downward. After tumbling head over heels for a few feet, I come to rest abruptly — jarringly — against a tree. With a groan, and using the tree as support, I stand carefully. My body is sore all over with bits of skin scraped from every exposed area. I hurt everywhere, but my relief at being free of the Buddha is so great, my pains are forgotten. It must have rained in the last few hours, since my trip down the hill was softened by old growth and mud. What a mess.

Bruised, battered, and filthy, I look a sight, but I'm out and that's all that's important. It's dark but there's a partial moon throwing light, and the stars are out. Accustomed to the darkness of the cave, the night seems almost bright. I make my way down the hillside. Knowing where Adrien and I are staying, I'm confident I can find my way back the two and a half miles to our hotel. Is that the correct destination? Should I attempt to make my way to the front of the Buddha? Might Adrien wait for me there? It's been hours since I went in the water, and the park must be closed. I look back in the direction I came with indecision. Would Adrien have gone to the hotel? Might the authorities be holding him for his involvement with me and my disappearance at the Buddha? I know nothing about the laws in China.

With nowhere else to go and not knowing what to do, I make my way to our hotel. Hopefully, he'll be there and we can regroup.

Continuing to walk, I keep my eyes open for a road or other point of reference, my sight on the moon to set my direction. My hand swings by my side and as it bumps into my leg, the weight in my pocket draws my attention. The metal piece has become forgotten in my fight to get out of the cave. Stopping, with a wince of pain, I shove my bloody, dirty hand into my pocket and pull out the object. It's barely visible in the darkness but I'm relieved it's real and I still have it. I push it back in my pocket and head out to find my way back to the hotel.

It's a long, tender walk to the hotel in my socks, but once I find a road it becomes easier. My clothes are sodden and dirty, the mud flaking off as it dries in areas. My hair hangs in filthy spikes that drip water, insuring I stay at an uncomfortable level of damp. Every once in a while, a full-body shiver racks my frame, but for the most part, the walk keeps me warm. A few cars pass, but when their lights become visible, I step out of sight. Something tells me not to be seen — will I be arrested? Am I in danger? Or just paranoid? Right now, my trust is only in Adrien, if I can locate him.

When arriving at the hotel, the shadows of a stand of trees keep me hidden while I study the area. It's well-lit, and there isn't anyone outside. Cautiously, I walk to our room and it hits me: my key is in the zippered pocket of my jacket — the jacket I handed to Adrien before jumping from the ferry.

Okay. A key. With a deep breath in and out, I give myself a moment to try to think what I'm going to say to the night man on duty to explain my appearance if Adrien isn't here. I figure I'll cross that bridge when I get to it, and with a step up to the door, I knock. Seconds later, the door is wrenched open.

"Ellen!" Adrien pauses in the doorway with a stunned look on his face. How can he even recognize me? I'm covered in mud and know I smell foul. By now, I've become immune to my own stench, but my condition doesn't seem to matter to him as he rushes to me and pulls me into his embrace. With his comforting touch and the sure knowledge I've made it back, my body collapses into itself. I've been able to keep going by not thinking — just acting. Now, I'm here and safe, and my adrenaline flows out of my body like someone opened a valve.

"Come, come, my dear," Adrien says with his arm around me, directing me into the room. He leads me to a chair, and as I ease into it, he closes and locks the door.

"Ellen. Oh, Ellen. I had hoped, but I can't begin to believe you're here. When you jumped off the ferry...well, my dear, I almost had a heart attack." He fusses about me like a mother hen, flittering here and there.

"Could I have a drink of water?" My brain touches on the irony of the desire for water when, not so long ago, I almost drowned.

"Of course. Of course." Adrien practically runs into the bathroom and soon reappears with a glass of wonderful, clean water.

"Thank you, Adrien," I say softly. Each time my voice croaks out, I hardly recognize its rumble. It sounds as if I've swallowed broken glass. Taking the cup with hands that quake, I sip the water. It's cool and refreshing. I look at him as he sits on the end of the bed, watching me.

"Let's get you cleaned up and then we can talk, shall we?"

I open my mouth to speak but must clear my throat before any words come out. "I can't begin to describe how welcome a hot shower would be." With a quick scan of the room, I see my boots and jacket laid out on the table. Rising a bit painfully, I grab what's needed from my suitcase, along with my boots, and head into the bathroom.

"Get yourself cleaned up and let me know when you're ready. Perhaps we'll order some food before we talk."

"That would be lovely, Adrien. Thank you. I won't be long."

He nods his head and turns away only to turn back to

face me. "I'm very relieved to have you back, Ellen. You had me worried."

"I'm sorry I worried you. I'll see you in a moment."

He nods, and I shut the door.

Standing with my back against the bathroom door, I heave a sigh and wrinkle my nose, catching a whiff of the scent that comes off me.

"Shower," I mumble to myself. "You really need a shower, Ellen."

I peel off my clothing and drop it, making a squishy sound when it impacts the floor. Bared to the skin, I walk into the shower and turn it on hot. Standing unmoving, I watch as the steam from the shower fills the small room. I'm having trouble believing I've made it back to the hotel and Adrien. I expect to come out of a stupor and still be drowning in the river or trapped in the tunnel. Though I'm afraid to believe this is real, I'm happy to accept the shower. It's hot, cleansing, and rejuvenating. Is there anything better than a hot shower? I bask under the spray for what seems a long time and allow the water to rinse away much of the dirt. It puddles and swirls around my feet like angry storm clouds before being pulled down the drain. Soon, I grab my shampoo and scrub my hair three times before it's clean. A little conditioner and a ton of soap, and I'm human again. My hands and the bottoms of my feet are throbbing. I towel-dry my hair, and after I run a brush through it, I spend some time slathering lotion on. Head to toe, I now smell faintly of vanilla.

The bathroom mirror is clear and I study my reflection. "You did it, Ellen. You're alive and well, girl."

Turning from my image, I grab clean underwear, jeans, and a T-shirt. Moving quickly now, I get dressed and pick up my dirty clothes to dump them on the sink. I remove the swastika piece from my jeans and drop it into the front pocket of my clean pants. Reaching for the door knob, I hesitate. Something is off. I don't know what — it's too quiet.

With a turn of the knob and a pull, the door opens. It creaks ominously and swings on its hinges. Did it do that before? I don't recall hearing the sound. Was I not aware, or has the atmosphere now affected the building?

Across the room, three men stand with Adrien. All four look at me, but no one speaks. Funny, but the first thing I note is they're all in suits. Dark suits. One man has Adrien's upper arm in a tight fist. He holds him so his shoulder is wrenched and Adrien is forced to stand on his tip-toes to accommodate what is surely a painful position. This man has a gun in his other hand and has it pointed at Adrien's head. A line of blood runs from Adrien's lip, and his mouth is swollen. *What happened while I was in the shower?* Another man stands on the opposite side slightly behind them, and a third man is in front. The two in back are like negative images of each other: one's white-blond, and the other has blue-black hair. Their suits fit them well and seem to be tailored specifically for them, emphasizing the fact they're large guys — like body builders. My eyes move from the men surrounding Adrien to the man in front. I study him as he appears to be studying me. Although he's smaller in stature, he's more than physically different. He's intelligent. He looks at me through crafty eyes covered by heavy brows, and projects a condescending, arrogant attitude.

"Come out, Ms. Thompson." He steps forward, gesturing to indicate I should exit the bathroom and have a seat. "Please, come out and join us. We have much to discuss."

His voice is low and breathy. His eyes sparkle with an inner excitement.

Adrien is plainly scared and though we're in danger, this makes me angry. *Why won't they leave us alone?* I should be more afraid, and maybe soon will be, but for right now I'm resentful. Are these guys part of the mysterious Guild? The unethical side in this search for the Guardian, that Adrien told me about? The two men on either side of Adrien are clearly hired muscle—they're bulls in human form.

Stepping forward again, the third man holds my attention. He's short, an inch or two under my height, and looks comfortable in this unconventional situation. I scrutinize him and immediately realize the true threat lies here. Here is the brain of the operation, the zealot. A man fueled by passion and ideals is dangerous, especially if he has no ethics or morals to govern his choices.

I break his gaze and look toward Adrien. He gives little shakes of his head to try to warn me off. With a deep breath for strength, I step into the room.

Stopping me with a lift of his hand, the small man says, "Before you sit and we talk, Ms. Thompson, please give me what you found in the Buddha." He moves toward me and extends his hand. I stare at his open palm and back to his face with his weak chin. I glance at Adrien again. His eyes are open wide and he's shaking his head. My gaze moves from him back to the man.

"I don't know what you're talking about. I don't have anything and was never in a Buddha." Keeping a blank look on my face, the swastika weight burns a hole against my leg.

"Now, now, Ms. Thompson," he states in his wheezy voice, pushing his fingers through his slicked-back hair. "I hate to resort to violence but I will have Mr. Bernard beaten until I get what I want." As he says this, he gestures in Adrien's direction. "He's just a pawn. You're the big fish. Cooperate and you will both be allowed to go free."

Is this guy for real? He's seen too many movies. I give him a condescending smile of my own. "You assume an emotional attachment that doesn't exist. I can't give you something I don't have, and no matter how much you harm Adrien, that fact won't change."

"Well, that is a dilemma, now isn't it, Ms. Thompson?" He gives the men who hold Adrien a small nod.

My whole body tenses for the expected violence and I roll forward on the balls of my feet in anticipation of a fight, but they don't do anything other than pull Adrien by us. The men open our hotel door and forcibly move him across the drive and into a black SUV. *Was that vehicle there before?*

"Come, Ms. Thompson."

I start as the man puts his hand on my elbow to direct me out the door. I didn't realize he'd gotten that close.

"Where are we going? What about my things?" Can he be distracted or overpowered? Should I make a break for it? How will Adrien get free?

He chuckles, shakes his head, and looks at me with a tender expression—like we're old friends and I've just said something funny. "I'll need the object you hold to tell you where we're going. Your things will be packed and will follow."

"Who are you?"

"You may call me Stephen."

We move to the drive as the vehicle with Adrien speeds away. A black Mercedes sedan pulls up; Stephen opens the door and indicates for me to get in. *Do I have a choice?* My gaze moves from him back to the open hotel door and around into the night, wishing I knew what to do. When I catch his eye, he gives me a small smirk, patiently waiting for me to accept the situation. Resigned, I slide into the back seat. It's a beautiful car, well-appointed with leather seats and all the extras — Gilded Cage and all that. He shuts the door with a finality that echoes in my bones, and as he walks around the car to enter from the other side, a moment of panic surges. My breath becomes jerky, heart races, and sweat beads my upper lip. I barely stop myself from flinging open the door and running for all I'm worth. Only two things stop me. One is Adrien. Where have they taken him and what will they do to him if I run? That, and the fact I'm in freakin' China. Without money or papers, both of which are in my room supposedly to follow shortly, I have no way out of this country and no way to exist in this country. Right now, these men look like my only option.

*****

Where's Adrien? Have they hurt him? Was there another solution besides capitulation in this situation?

In another carefree situation, I'd enjoy a ride in a private jet. It is an extremely luxurious way to travel. This situation, however, changes everything. My seat is toward the back, where they've left me. The chair — lounger, really — is large and plush. Stephen and another man sit toward the front and speak in quiet tones I can't quite make out, but occasionally, they turn and look my direction.

I stare out the window at the rolling clouds and my

mind drifts back to the ride to the airport and my interaction with the man in charge, Stephen.

*****

In the sedan, my body is tense. Out the darkened windows are vague shapes of buildings, but my mind is on my situation and possible solutions. Stephen shifts next to me, causing a squeak of the leather seats. With a glance in his direction, I note he's staring at me with raised eyebrows, his expression full of expectancy.

"So, Ms. Thompson? Where will we be going?" His voice grates on my nerves. Everything about this man grates on my nerves.

Saying nothing, I study him. His patience level is impressive and freakish as he returns my stare. The big question is what to do. It seems the only way forward is to share the metal fragment. Backwards is unavailable and sitting still isn't going to get any of us—myself and Adrien included—out of this.

With a slight shift, I reach gingerly into my front pocket, my hands and fingers still torn and painful. Stephen sits forward and tracks my every move like a dog waiting for a treat. With a pause, I take a moment to run my fingertip over the smooth side of the piece and long for another idea, some solution. Is this the way to go? With a glance at Stephen, I pull the metal from my pocket and open my hand to him. He releases an audible exhale but doesn't attempt to take it.

"An Akan gold weight."

Huh? I think. *A what, what?*

He reaches out and runs his finger over the weight and

in an almost unintentional error, he continues and runs his finger over my hand and wrist. A cold shiver of revulsion runs down my spine, but I don't pull away. I watch him closely.

Stephen drops his hand and holds my gaze as he takes a cell phone from an inner pocket of his jacket. "Tell the pilot to ready the plane. Set a flight plan for Ghana, Africa."

He puts the phone away and asks, "May I hold it, Ms. Thompson?"

Suddenly feeling less cooperative, I close my fingers around the weight and put my hands together on my lap. I scrutinize him, and as his gaze shifts from my hand to my eyes, his own eyes glisten with appreciation. He gives me a small smile. A heavy foreboding weighs. I really don't want to attract this man—this horrible, scary man.

"Come," he says. "It's time to board. We'll talk more during the flight."

*****

A burst of sunlight reflects off the billowy white clouds, and I close my eyes and shift from the window of the plane. With a weary suspicion, I watch as Stephen approaches. He has a close eye on me. He's avaricious of his new possession.

With a sigh of satisfaction, he sits in the seat next to mine and turns toward me. "So, Ellen. May I call you Ellen?" With a small nod from me, he continues. "Ellen. I'll need to see the gold weight now. We're almost to Ghana, but there are many towns and many buildings within those towns. I need to see what else is on the weight to indicate where we're to go."

As he talks, my mind imagines the weight, the intricate

75

etchings on the back side. I'm sure these are what Stephen wants to see. What will they tell him? He sits next to me, too close, and patiently watches. This guy's like a cobra and he gives me the creeps.

"Where's Adrien?"

Stephen shakes his head and murmurs, "Mr. Bernard is no longer your concern, Ellen. You're with me now."

Where is his mind? What fantasy has he conjured in his pointed little head to justify our abductions? How can it be used to my advantage?

"I can't be my best if I'm worried about Adrien. If you'd let me see him, talk to him, I'm sure I'll be able to concentrate on our quest and do my best for you." Reaching across the seat, I lay my hand on his forearm. His chin drops to his chest as he focuses on my touch. "Please, Stephen." I try to soften my tone, to project whatever he needs to allow him to give me what I want. "I want to help you, but I have daughterly feelings for Adrien and I don't want him to come to harm."

Placing his hand over mine, Stephen catches my eye and holds my gaze. "I understand. You're a woman of deep feelings; that's why you're such an essential part of this." At his overly warm touch, my stomach makes a little jump and I swallow a wave of nausea. I leave my hand under his and on his arm for another moment while he gazes at me fondly.

Icky, I think with an inner grimace. *I'm gonna need a hot shower.*

Slowly, I pull my hand away and sit back. "So may I speak with Adrien? May I see him?"

Stephen pulls out his phone and pushes a button. A second later he says, "Put him on," and hands it to me.

I take the phone. That was pretty easy, and anything that

simple puts me on edge. As I put the phone to my ear, my eyes track him with a steady gaze. He straightens his jacket, sits back, crosses his legs, and drapes an arm over the back of my seat.

"Hello?" Adrien's voice comes over the phone. He sounds tired, but it's as if he's next door. Of course, next door would be outside at 40,000 feet.

"Adrien! Adrien, it's Ellen!" Sitting forward, I curl into myself. The phone is held to my ear with both hands. "Adrien, are you all right?"

"Ellen! My dear, where are you? How are you?"

With a subtle shift, Stephen sits forward and places his hand on my shoulder. My body arches and I jerk to the side to give him a glare of reproach. I pull away to stand as surprise fills my mind. Listening to Adrien's voice in my ear, I spin to stare at Stephen. The look in his eyes absorbs my attention: he's pleased. The bastard is pleased I rejected him just now. So far, I've gotten what I'm after but this psycho is going to warrant an extremely watchful eye. For the first time, there's a sharp sting of fear. It's become painfully obvious—Stephen is not someone I want to deal with. How can I hope to manipulate a mind I can't even understand?

There's not a lot of room to maneuver, but I need to walk, to move. My mind spins and can't land on a plan that will see Adrien and me safe.

"Ellen? Ellen, are you all right? They haven't hurt you?" His voice is worried and overloud.

"No, Adrien. I'm fine, I'm fine. Do you know where you are?"

"No, my dear. I'm sorry. I was in an aircraft, but now I have been moved to a building somewhere. I don't even know for certain what country I am in."

"I'm going to fix this." I head back toward Stephen. "I'll see you soon. Stay strong." With a push of the end button, I hand the phone to him. "I'm going to need him at the location we end up at, you know that, right?"

"Hmm," he says with a cock of his head. "Need? I don't believe you need anyone for you to be successful, but I want us to work well together. I believe I can arrange to have Mr. Bernard transferred to our location. Of course, I'll need to see the gold weight to know where that is."

"All right, Stephen. All right. We'll call this a give and take, shall we?" I reach into my front pants pocket and pull out the weight. It feels even heavier in my grip, and I don't want to give it up but drop it in his outstretched palm.

With a huge, satisfied smile, he clenches the weight in his fist and stands up way within my bubble of space. Instinctively, I step back, and he gives me a grin.

"Ellen," he cajoles. "You're going to need to get used to my proximity. I have a feeling you and I are going to be very close friends." This said, he reaches out and tucks a stray piece of hair behind my ear.

Chapter 7

We're traveling down a dirt road with only two silent men in the front seat for company. There's an abundance of trees on either side, but they're different from any I've seen before — tall, dark green, with their foliage in the top third of their mass. They remind me of the bushes in my parents' yard after the grasshoppers have been at them. People move along the roadside, and by their ethnicity and clothing, they announce Africa to me. They're beautiful, and their clothing is vibrantly colored with primary colors in swirls and patches. Many of the women have baskets nestled within coils atop their heads. My own head swings almost painfully fast to track as we pass an elephant. An *elephant*! I've seen one in a circus and on TV, but to see one standing on the road — extraordinary! I've never been to Africa.

Outside our vehicle it's dusty and hot, but the interior is cool, bordering on cold. The evening sky is heavy with clouds and when a window is cracked, I smell the threat of rain.

"Where are we going, Stephen?"

"We'll be there soon," he replies evasively.

After leaving China and landing at the airport in Africa, we were met by another black SUV, identical to the other. Stephen quickly hustled me into it. I guess I should be thankful they didn't place a black bag over my head or something. I've yet to hear our companions speak; I don't even know if they can. The two men are part of the cookie-cutter group surrounding Stephen. They're dressed in dark suits and give nothing away. *Who are these guys? Who have I hooked up with?*

In the SUV, we travel through the growing dark of Africa. I address Stephen again, unable to contain my concern about Adrien's whereabouts. "Where's Adrien?"

"He'll meet us at our destination."

"Which is where?"

Stephen shifts toward me and brings his hands together. He interlaces his fingers and taps his pursed lips thoughtfully with the index ones. With a small, private smile, he watches me, and my eyes grow wider; very quickly, I become uncomfortable. Turning to look out the window of the vehicle, I watch the country pass by. How am I supposed to deal with this guy? He's like no one I've ever met before. Crazy.

Seriously bat-shit crazy.

We continue to drive into the setting sun. The horizon is hidden by the trees but still the sky is stunning. It's full of yellows and oranges, and I wish I could be on the Serengeti, with no worries, to witness the dazzling end of this day. My pleasure in its beauty is almost smothered by the presence of my companions and the situation I'm in. It's a mental exercise to concentrate on the spectacle of nature. To find something to appreciate.

Losing myself in the view, I lift a water bottle to my lips to drink, and when I wipe the excess from my mouth, a shiver snakes up my spine. With my fingers at my mouth, I glance over my shoulder at Stephen to realize he's tracking my every movement. I'm like a bug under a glass, but a coveted bug, a very coveted bug. How will I get away from this guy? Will I be able to save myself and Adrien? And really, who is Stephen? How do I find out? Will Adrien be able to tell me anything?

*****

The sun drops behind the edge of the world as we pull into a small village. It's brilliant and abrupt, like someone blew out a flame. As we drive forward, there aren't any people around. Are they in for the night? The village feels deserted. It's unnaturally quiet, without even a barking dog to break the silence. Moving to the middle of the village, the vehicle we're in circles a center court to stop in front of an odd structure. There are two other vehicles parked here, but both appear to be empty. Looking out the window, I study the building intently. From one perspective, it looks like the other buildings, only taller. It has no windows and sports an extremely pitched, thatched roof. However, because we circled the area and saw it from all sides, I know it's three buildings put together to create one. There's a doorway on one side and what appears to be reliefs etched into the wood walls. Standing out sharply against the pale wood is an alligator and a man and woman. These images are duplications of the images on the gold weight. Now I know why we're here, but not what to expect.

My attention is drawn behind me when Stephen opens the other door and exits the vehicle. The two clones in the front seat follow his lead, but I'm uncertain if I'm to follow or stay. The decision is made for me when, after speaking with the two men, Stephen opens my door.

"Well, Ellen. Are you ready?"

Ready for what?

Tentatively, I place my hand on the door and step into the evening air. It's gotten cooler and the threat of a storm has become a promise as thunder rolls in the distance.

With a hand on my elbow, Stephen leads me toward the doorway in the building. A small breeze kicks up and blows my bangs off my forehead. With it comes the smell of rain.

Through sheer force of will, I don't pull away, but Stephen's touch gives me the creeps and my skin literally crawls. I swing my eyes back and forth and look for anything, any information to tell me what to expect. Two men have spread out on both sides and stand ready. Again, I ask myself, *ready for what?* We near and pass them. They have their guns pulled and hold them pointed down as they study us and the area.

When we get to the building, Stephen steps forward onto

a platform to push the door inward. It opens with a loud screech of wood on metal. I glance behind us, expecting the noise to draw someone, but the village remains deserted. Looking inside, the room beyond is dark, but as I take two steps up to enter the structure, an inner courtyard becomes visible and is silhouetted in the light from a rising moon. Figures stand inside, a couple mill about, but it's too dark to identify them. The floor resonates hollowly with my footsteps. I stand at the edge of the room and look across the small courtyard at the other buildings. They're in a triangular design, with open fronts and steps down to the dirt. Adrien stands in the courtyard, and with a smile of relief and a small gasp, I start forward only to find my upper arm gripped in a steel fist. My breath catches, and I look first to my arm, knowing there'll be a bruise in the morning, and then to Stephen's eyes.

"You will wait and do exactly as I say."

I'm still as a statue except for the movement of my chest with my deep breaths as I watch Stephen. I'm not good at taking orders, but to risk Adrien is foolish, and I don't trust this man to not simply shoot him.

"You will solve this unknown portion of my puzzle and when you do, you shall be rewarded with Mr. Bernard's life." With an intent look, Stephen raises an eyebrow. "Do we have an understanding, Ellen?"

"Yes, Stephen. I understand you completely." I say what he wants, but by no stretch of the imagination do I believe he will willingly free Adrien—or me for that matter. We're going to have to free ourselves.

"Good. Very good." With a small nod of his head, he releases my arm. He reaches up, slides his hand under my hair, and pushes it back from my collar and nape. I try to control it, but my body gives a little shiver of reaction, and he chuckles softly.

"If you would consider the courtyard and tell me what you see."

I look up and out, glance left and right.

"What do you see?"

"A triangular-shaped courtyard. Three buildings with faces open to the yard, two steps up to the buildings. There are paintings on each of the buildings, and what looks to be possibly instruments in the one, although it's too dark to tell for certain."

Stephen stands next to me and looks in each of the directions as I talk, nodding his head slowly.

"There are two of your men in the courtyard with Adrien, and a tree..." I stop and peer at the tree from where I stand. "May I approach the tree?"

Chuckling again softly, he states in his wispy voice, "Why of course. You're not a prisoner. We're partners; you may go where you choose."

Uh huh. I know for a fact this is a lie but I don't argue with him. I step down the stairs and although I want to go to Adrien, talk to him, make certain he's all right, I only glance his direction and continue to the tree. It's a narrow tree trunk, about twelve inches around, and the top has been cut so it ends in a V of branches. Within the V sits a painted pot. The pot has a soft illumination from an undiscernible source. With a tentative touch, I reach out to the tree trunk to find it's warm; not warm like with the heat of the day, warm like a living being. I swear it pulses under my fingertips.

"Why is the pot lit? Is it part of a ritual or something?"

Stephen walks around me to the other side of the tree and, looking up, inspects the pot. After a moment, he drops his gaze to peer at me.

"What do you mean lit? What does it look like to you, exactly?"

Ah, shit, I think. *Add this freakin' pot to my list with the kachina and lotus.*

Ignoring his question, I say, "I'm going to need my gold weight back, Stephen."

"*Your* gold weight?" He shakes his head at me with raised eyebrows. "Don't you mean *my* gold weight?"

No, that's not what I meant, but with a direct stare, I say, "*The* gold weight. I'm going to need it returned to me."

Apparently, he decides to not argue this point and reaches into his inner jacket pocket to retrieve the weight. Giving me a warning stare, he gently sets the weight in my palm. I turn it over and focus on it. The wash of relief that floods over my body by simply having it back in my possession almost overwhelms me, and I take a deep breath. Suddenly, an image of the golden leaf jumps into my head. Where is it? Did it get packed with my belongings and brought to Africa? Did they find it and understand what it is?

With a step back from the tree, I turn to Stephen and ask, "Where are my belongings?"

"What?" he asks with apparent confusion at the abrupt change in subject.

"I want to know where my stuff is."

"That is unimportant at this juncture, Ellen."

"Unimportant to you, perhaps, but not to me. They're *my* things, and I want to know where they are. You promised me everything would be packed and would follow me and now I want to know where — "

"*All right!*" he yells, effectively silencing my deliberate rant before I'd even gotten warmed up. "All your things, and those of Mr. Bernard, are in the vehicle we came in. Satisfied?" he asks with a tilt of his head and lift of his brows.

"Yes. Thank you." Abruptly, knowing the quick change will throw him off, I step forward, reach up, and drop the gold weight into the pot in the tree. Instantaneously, the illumination, which apparently is only visible to me, shines brighter and then goes out.

"What are you doing?" Stephen snarls at me, starting forward, but just then the earth screams. There's a shifting underfoot and he stumbles to the side, catching himself with his arms thrown out. It's as if a waking dragon is shaking dirt from its back.

Grabbing onto the tree trunk, I hold myself steady and look across the courtyard. The two men with Adrien have moved backward into the dubious protection of one of the buildings. Both have their weapons drawn, and there is real fear on all three of their faces. The tree shudders as Stephen uses it to stand upright when another giant convulsion shakes the earth.

"*What is this?*" he yells. "What did you do?"

Even if I knew, which I don't, I wouldn't tell him. In answer, I look out across the courtyard and watch in astonishment as the dirt shifts and the center of the yard begins to sink.

What the hell?

With a revolving counter-clockwise motion, the center of the courtyard rotates and slowly drops below ground level. Dirt and rocks skitter and bounce as they spill downward into the opening gap. Another shudder rocks the area, and an unearthly screeching sound has all of us cringing and covering our ears with our hands. As suddenly as it began, it ends in silence. A silence that's only marred by the tinkling of rocks and debris falling into the hole that now sits in the center of the courtyard.

Cautiously, dropping my hands from my ears and moving away from the tree, I approach the pit in the middle of the yard. Looking back at Stephen, I ask, "Do you have a flashlight?"

Turning to one of the two men, he says, "Get some light!"

The man turns and hustles up and out the doorway, returning momentarily with another man and not only a couple flashlights, but three portable lanterns. The flashlights are handed to Stephen and with some obvious trepidation, the men set the lanterns up around the hole. Soon the entire area is awash with harsh, unnatural light. Stephen slowly approaches me and, handing over one of the flashlights, moves back from the hole.

I glance at Adrien, but with the courtyard and its gaping hole between us, I can't get any information or impression from him. Approaching the pit to stand at the edge, I look down. A spiral stairway leads into darkness and silence. *I'm really glad I'm not claustrophobic* is a thought that keeps occurring through this...adventure? Experience? Quest? What's with all the small, dark, enclosed spaces? Taking a deep breath and turning on the flashlight, I take the first step down.

"Go with her," Stephen says to one of the men, but I ignore them and continue.

Reaching the bottom, I pause, and using the illumination of the flashlight in a sweeping arc, I look at the entire area and then back the way I've come. There's a packed dirt floor about forty feet under the surface. Everything smells of the earth; airless and musty, it fills my senses. In front of me, three passageways open. They all look exactly alike. Other than the flat floor, they're rounded and about six feet in height. My head fills with a disquieting image of a huge worm creating them by eating its way through the dirt and rock.

Great, Ellen. Now is not the time to let your imagination run away with you.

Standing still, I peer down first one tunnel and, shifting slightly, down another and then another. In my nostrils is the smell of the soil and some other intangible quality I can't place. It reminds me of a mixture of hot tar and cooking meat. As I stand there, confused and not knowing which way to go, one of Stephen's men climbs down the steps behind me. With a scowl, I turn and shine the light on him, looking him up and down. He puts a hand up in front of his eyes, but I don't lower the light. He's one of the guys from the vehicle, the one who came back with the lanterns, but there's no comradery because of our time spent together. If anything, I'm more uncomfortable with him for the same reason. He appears edgy as his eyes sweep quickly back and forth, and he has his weapon in his hand. A combination that isn't helping me relax.

"Ellen." A voice comes from above, and glancing up, I see Stephen standing on the edge of the pit. "You come back with what we need or Mr. Bernard will be the one to suffer. Eric will accompany you to ensure your return." With a dirty look, I barely suppress the impulse to give him the bird. I'm getting pretty sick and tired of Stephen.

Turning away from the henchman behind me, I select the tunnel to the right for no good reason and head into it. My steps and the steps of my shadow echo faintly down and back in the dim passageway. It's not long before a feeling of anxiety begins to come over me and I have to consciously push the image of the dirt and rock surrounding us out of my head.

We haven't gone far when a secondary passage cuts across the one we're on. Stopping, I shine my light down one way and then the other. The beam of the flashlight dissipates a short distance from us, almost as if the quality of the air is changing. Our visibility is nil. Other than the sounds of our breathing and the scuff of our foot falls, the tunnels are utterly silent. The more time passes, the warmer it becomes, and breathing in the warm, dusty air takes effort. There are no signs to indicate which way to go, and I decide to stay on the main track, but the further we go the more erratic the tunnel is. It's crisscrossed multiple times with no rhyme or reason.

I glance back at Eric as he trails me and receive a blank stare. With a deep breath, I push my sweaty bangs off my forehead and run my fingers through my hair. Giving a small shake of my head in a fit of indecision, I turn back the way we came. After walking for what feels like miles, we're just as lost and there's no sign of the staircase. Somehow, we've become completely turned around.

Looking at the man with me, I ask, "Any ideas?" without any real hope of an answer.

My expectations are met when he returns my look with silence and empty eyes.

"Great." I turn around and continue, but it's become

painfully obvious we're in a massive underground labyrinth with no real hope of getting out without help.

*****

It's hot, stagnant, and dusty in the maze. Sweat pools under my breasts and runs down my back. Time stands still with the never-changing, never-ending passages. The dust clings to my face, and Eric is in the same state. There're tracks of sweat running down the sides of his face, and I'm sure mine shows the same furrows in the dirt on my skin. *How long has it been?*

"You should have brought water," I say to him, mostly just to hear my voice but also to get some kind of reaction. Nothing. He's the most silent person I've ever been around. *Maybe he's mute*, I think. *Stephen would like that, being the only one to talk.*

After taking a few more turns that feel right at the time, we come to a juncture of tunnels and I decide to rest. Exhaustion and my aching legs, hips, and feet tell me I need to sit. I squat with my back against the wall and push my legs out in front of me. My muscles quiver slightly at the change in position and then relax.

The last few days have been trying, and I haven't had sufficient time to realign myself each time. Adrien coming out of nowhere, the encounter with a kachina, jetting off to China, almost drowning, walking miles in my socks, getting kidnapped and taken to Africa, and now I'm lost in an underground maze with a silent, lethal man. *My life's an adventure a minute.*

With curiosity, I watch as Stephen's man joins me on the floor. He sighs and leans his head back against the tunnel but doesn't volunteer any help or conversation.

Looking from him, I glance first down one tunnel and then the next. How long will the battery on my flashlight hold out? I'm afraid to shut it off for fear it won't turn back on when needed. Without the artificial light, we'll be in pitch-black. I try to relax, taking a deep pull of air, and decide to shut my eyes for just a moment and catch my breath. Maybe an idea will come to me. In my relaxing mind, the words circle: *truth and honesty are swept aside. Search deep and triumph well...*

*****

With a jolt upright from the wall, I realize I fell asleep. *What woke me?* Blinking quickly, I look toward my sidekick to see him shining his flashlight and looking with wide eyes into the tunnel we've come from.

Scritch. Scratch.

My heartbeat jumps. There. There it is again. Now hearing it, I know it's the sound that woke me.

Scritch. Scratch.

I rise to a crouch as Eric lumbers to his feet, both of us watching down the tunnel, our flashlights scanning the darkness. This is really not a great sound, and my mind pulls me back to the image of a huge worm eating its way through the tunnel. And eating anything it comes across.

We need to get moving. Standing fully, I start to back away from the tunnel where the noise emanates. Eric quickly follows my lead. We scan into the dark, waiting for something to jump out. Luckily, there aren't any more noises. Facing forward, we head down the tunnel with a quick, shuffling gait.

We're going nowhere fast when just out of the edge of the flashlight's circle, something black and indistinct catches my vision. My footsteps slow and I squint, but it disappears as soon as my eyes lock on it. We move forward again, but as before, there's only a momentary image of the edge of it. As we approach, it advances at the same rate of speed, just fast enough to stay out of the light. Curious, I pick up my pace and move the light further out in front of us but can't catch it.

Soon, frustrated and tiring, I stop. Eric, coming up fast behind me, fails to notice my abrupt halt and collides into me, knocking me to the ground. Falling, I flail out, pin-wheeling my arms, and the flashlight flies from my hand to land in the tunnel with a tinny sound, spinning wildly forward. The light flashes around and around. Looking up from my prone position, I see the tunnel in the whirling light—light, dark, light, dark—as the phantom moves forward.

The apparition steps into the rotating light on multiple long legs. Can this possibly be right? My body and mind are frozen in awe and fear. At the turn, in a bend of the tunnel, stands a spider. A spider as tall as my waist. Short tufts of reddish-hued hair cover its black body. It moves closer, appearing to walk on its tiptoes in its spidery way, as the flashlight finishes its final rotation. I want to jump up and run screaming down the tunnel, but I'm frozen. My limbs won't move—even my eyes are frozen as I stare at the form coming into view in the dusty half-light of the lantern. It makes little sound as the legs move, inching closer and closer. What is it? How can it be living down in this maze of tunnels? I don't even want to know what it eats. When it's within a few feet of me, it turns its head to look down where I lay prostrate like an offering before it, and to my abject horror, I see it has a human face. It studies me through human eyes.

With a shriek that can be heard back in China, my brain shorts out due to a massive overload of terror and adrenaline that hits my system. I'm not thinking. Just running on pure animal impulse as I find myself on my feet and fleeing down the tunnel straight into Eric. His eyes widen with a look of astonishment as I catch him in the throat with my forearm. He grasps me around the waist, and we both go down. On top, I'm struggling for purchase and crawling up and over him, kicking out as I go. He catches my ankle just as I'm free and with a mighty heave pulls me back to grab me around the waist.

Standing easily, even with my weight, he spins me around, scanning my face.

"What? What's going on?"

I'm not thinking and past talking. With terror-filled glances back down the tunnel, I kick and punch at him in a vain attempt to be released. It doesn't matter there's nowhere to go; I need to not be here. He has his head down and a powerful grip on me. I'm unable to get him to release me no matter how much or how often I pummel him with my fists. Out of desperation, my aim changes and I go for his eyes. As my fingers, like talons, reach for him, he lets go of my waist, grabs my wrists, and spins me to wrench my arms behind my back. I've gone feral, thrashing against him as he pushes me face-first into the side of the tunnel.

"Stop it. Calm down!"

But I can't. I can't. I continue to kick at his shins and throw my head back in my struggle for freedom. My own grunts and whimpers are all I hear, and I may go over the edge into insanity if he doesn't release me. But, the body can only maintain panic for so long, and I soon wear down. I don't have a reserve of energy to continue this level of frenzy. With a last few futile kicks, my head hangs, resting against the wall as I take great gulps of the hot, dry air. Even though I'm still, Eric continues to hold my wrists as if he's afraid I'll try and bolt again—I don't think I can. I'm spent.

Rolling my head on my shoulders, my sight moves down the tunnel and a small moan escapes my lips, for the man-spider still blocks the way. My body gives a full shudder, and my eyes are glued to its face. As I watch, it blinks and watches me back.

"Oh God, oh God," I weep as a cold shiver arches down my spine.

"What? What has you freaking out?"

Sanity must be returning when it registers my companion can talk.

Shaking my head to clear it, I ask him, "Can't you see it?"

"See what?"

See what? Closing my eyes, I wish with all my being it'll be gone when I open them. I want to be able to say, "See what?"

It's not to be, though. Staring at the man-spider, I try and get my logy brain to work. If Eric can't see it, then either it's a hallucination, a dream, or my list of unexplainable phenomenon just gained another line. It's not moving, simply standing and blocking the tunnel. Could we walk through it? Would it move, or just disappear? And what good would that do us? I'm going to die down here with only Eric for company.

Okay, I think. *What does it want and how do I figure this out?* The words come back to me again: *truth and honesty are swept aside. Search deep...* Well, we're certainly deep. Is that what it means? Deep within or deep in the earth...or in deep shit?

"You can let go of me now. I'm okay."

He seems disinclined to believe me and asks, "Are you sure? You pack a hell of a punch. I don't want to have to chase you down this dark tunnel."

"Yes, I'm sure." Part of me is happy I connected my fist with his face and part of me is embarrassed I so totally lost it.

Slowly, releasing my wrists, he steps back a couple paces and raises his hands, palms out. My arms drop to my sides, and pulling them around front, I rub my wrists, which are bruised from his hold.

"So, what had you freaking out?"

"Nothing. Nothing, I'm better now. Let's continue on."

I turn toward the man-spider and take a step, then another. When I'm within two feet of it, my stomach turning over in anticipation of not knowing what is going to happen and the creepy factor of that human getting my dread rolling again, it turns and moves away from me with a distinctive spider gait. It's large enough that one set of legs reaches on the wall as the other sets move across the floor. It's perfectly silent.

Okay. It's now or never. As we follow, I stoop to retrieve my flashlight from the floor. Continuing to track it, I hope we're not being led to an immense web in the middle of this labyrinth. Maybe it can keep its food fresh for the years it takes for another meal to show up. This is so not fun, and nightmares are going to haunt me for years. If I live through it.

We continue to move through the tunnels, following the spider in a seemingly random pattern. Time is passing, I'm sure, but it's as if we're in a time warp—a Groundhog Day situation. The only discernable indication of the passage of time and space is the fatigue in my body. *How far have we gone?* Eric hasn't spoken again. He hasn't even questioned where we're going.

I don't realize my feet are dragging until my toe hooks on something and I'm pitched forward. Before I can catch myself, there's a steadying hand on my arm. With wide eyes, I look down at the hand and then up into Eric's face. He stares at me but says nothing. It's then I notice he has a bruise under his eye. I guess I do pack a punch.

"I'm sorry I hit you," I say with genuine regret.

He nods and scans my face. "You're okay now?" he asks, and for the first time I realize he has an accent. For a moment, my mind is filled with images of windswept fjords and large Viking men.

"Yes. I'm fine." I turn away from him, and he releases my arm as we continue down the tunnel.

Soon after, the man-spider turns a corner. Following him with Eric following me, I turn the corner and see the tunnel open into a room. The chamber is covered in spider webbing, but in the center is a pedestal, and on the pedestal is a reed basket.

"Stay here," I say to Eric and move into the room.

My footsteps echo hollowly as I advance into the chamber. As soon as I near the pedestal, the man-spider steps into my path, effectively stopping me. With a feign to the right, he follows me; the same thing happens with a move to the left. It's not threatening, just persistent. I wonder again, *is the man-spider real? Can I walk right through him?*

In an effort to put my questions to the test, I walk forward, coming nearer and nearer to him. My skin tingles and the hair rises on the back of my neck. My senses are freaking out and my mind wants to shut down with the sheer strangeness of that human face and those eyes looking out at me from the body of a spider. With steely control, I move closer. One more step and one more. My eyes are on the spider as I move my foot to take a step, but my forward momentum is halted in place. I just racked my toe, knee, and nose on something — something I can't see. I place my hands on it. It's firm, solid, and slick like glass, but even this close, it's not visible. I look up and all around. I'm stopped in my tracks before I can get close enough to touch him, and I sure as hell can't walk through him. *What now?* I need to get to that pedestal and retrieve the basket. I don't know what might be in it, but after all the time spent in these tunnels, it's my prize.

Thinking furiously, I step backward. "Eric, when you look into this room, what do you see?"

His eyes bore into me and then his head pivots as he scans the area. "A bare room with a stone platform in the middle. There's some kind of basket sitting on the platform."

Okay. Well good. At least he can see the basket. I have an idea. "I'm going to need you to head into the room from one side and then move quickly toward the pedestal after you're partway in, okay? Do you understand?"

"Yes. Why?" With just a glance at his face, it's apparent his brain is working to figure out what's going on, and I can appreciate that.

"There's more going on here and I really can't explain

right now; maybe at another time I will. All I can tell you is I need your help, and I'm praying this will allow us to get out of here."

Nodding his head at me, he steps into the room and moves to the right along the wall. As he moves, the man-spider tracks him with his too-human eyes. Eric continues to move along the wall, but the man-spider shifts his gaze from him back to me. He doesn't appear to be enough of a threat and I appear as too much. Looking off the other way, I attempt to project an air of disinterest. Pretty soon I'll be freakin' whistling. This tactic seems to work, and with a small glance my way, his attention returns to Eric.

Truth and honesty are swept aside...

Inching farther into the room and coming closer to the intersection where he'll veer toward the basket, Eric glances at me and then bolts for the pedestal. With this abrupt movement, the man-spider darts toward him, leaving the path open for me. I waste no time as I dig in and make a dash straight for the basket. Out of the corner of my eye, I see the man-spider switch direction, and with unearthly speed he whirls toward me. His hairy body is set to bowl me over when I push off and make a flying leap for the basket, knocking it from the pedestal with my hand. Rolling with it in my arms, I come to my feet and heave the basket at Eric. "Eric, catch," I shout, and reversing direction, I make a wide swoop toward the door. The man-spider tracks the arc of the basket overhead and, spinning its body, heads after it. Eric catches the basket and again I yell to him. "Drop it! Get to the door!" I give him credit as he obeys my shouted orders without question. The man-spider ignores him and skitters to the basket, turning it over with the tips of two of his front legs.

Truth and honesty are swept aside…

The hair on the nape of my neck stands as he moves and shifts. Stepping to the side, I allow Eric to rush past me and into the hallway. He turns to look in again as my attention is focused on the creature. Looking from the basket to me in the doorway, he seems to be… pleased? I step back near the arch, with the door framing me, and hold up what was taken from the basket. That face, that horrible human face in the spider body, smiles. He's still smiling at me as a stone slab falls to close the doorway.

I consider what just happened. Truth. Honesty. The opposite of them is subterfuge, deception. The use of your imagination. We needed to trick the man-spider to get the item. As this thought solidifies in my brain, everything whites out and new words appear:

Time rolls on, turns evermore.
Acceptance is approval, denial – rejection,
to embrace the chance, to glimpse through the veil.

In a momentary trance, the words absorb into my being. Like before, there is no understanding of what they mean, but unlike before, I'm now confident I'll figure it out.

With a slow blink, I awaken from my stupor. Inhaling, a cough shakes my frame and I stumble backward from the door and into Eric, who is wheezing in a breath. My eyes squint. The portal is gone. It doesn't look as if it ever existed. Gust and debris float around, and catching my breath is a battle. Each inhale causes a fit of coughing. With one hand on the wall and the other over my mouth, I see a defused light coming from down the corridor. A look of disbelief covers my face as I stand straight and look toward the illumination. Behind me, Eric has stopped in his tracks, too. We stand like statues and stare in amazement and shock. The radiance streaks through the air-borne dust like a beam from the heavens. We've been delivered.

Eric steps ahead of me and heads toward the light, his face dreamy, as if he can't believe what he's seeing. Stepping to follow him, my toe bumps into something on the dirt floor. Looking down, I see a few pieces of stone that were knocked loose when the doorway closed. Without questioning my judgment, I stoop and pick one up. It's big enough to over-fill my hand and has a hefty weight. I approach Eric and as he turns to look at me with a smile on his face, I whack him on the temple with the stone. He drops like one.

Okay. I feel a little guilty. By the end, he'd seemed as if he could be a kinda nice guy.

With a toss, the stone lands on the side of the tunnel, and I stand over him for a minute longer, watching him as he lies on his side gently breathing. It's good to know I haven't killed him. For a moment, the words drift in and out of my mind. *Time rolls on, turns evermore. Acceptance is approval, denial – rejection, to embrace the chance, to glimpse through the veil.* I put the question of the words aside and deal with the issue at hand.

With a quick motion, the object from the basket is slid down my shirt to catch at my pants. I squat beside Eric. Grasping his shoulder and giving him a good push, I shove him onto his back. His suit jacket flops open, and reaching into his shoulder harness, I take his firearm. The grip is big for me, but still, it feels good in my hand. I eject the magazine —

fully loaded—and slap it back in. I move the slide and take a quick look in the barrel to ensure a shell is racked. A quick check of his other pockets gifts me with a set of keys, a switchblade knife, and a phone. I leave the phone, having become paranoid about tracking devices. Standing, I pocket the keys and knife and stare down at Eric.

"Sorry, big guy. Maybe we'll meet again and I can return whatever favor might be owed."

Turning from him, I face the light. The dust is settling, and in the near distance, I make out the bottom of a stairway. Walking forward to stop at the bottom, I cock my head and concentrate, listening. At first, there's no sound, but then comes the hum of faint voices.

My first concern seems like a weird one. *Are these the same set of stairs?* On silent feet, I move up the stairway in a sideways motion. Keeping as low and quiet as possible, I peek over the edge at the top. Two men, recognizable as two of Stephen's, sit on a set of steps leading into one of the structures. They're visiting quietly and don't seem to be on guard. Relief washes over my brain like a balm, and with a sigh, my breathing comes easier. Rising slightly higher, I spin slowly around, scanning for anyone else; it's only then I notice Adrien lying across the courtyard wrapped in a blanket. His shoulders are uncovered and his head is propped on another blanket. He appears to be sleeping. Continuing my scan, I don't see Stephen anywhere.

Back in a squat below the edge on the stair, I fortify my resolve. *You can do this, Ellen. You will do this!* With my courage screwed securely in place, I pop back up to peer at the men again. Stepping up the stair, keeping silent, I take aim at the one on the right. A few seconds pass, but my finger won't move to the trigger and take the shot. My brain is failing to comply. The gun becomes heavy in my hands, and my arms quake. Is it really the weight of the gun causing my tremors, or what's in my sights? With calm breaths, I stare down the barrel of the gun. The man is a slightly out-of-focus figure beyond, but my head knows it's a human being—a living, breathing human being. With force, I ignore the image of him being blown apart by my weapon and the distress the image gives me. Maybe if he were trying to kill me or even threatening me, I could shoot him, but sitting there drinking what appears to be coffee and visiting with someone...I just can't do it.

I breath a small sigh and drop below the lip of the ground. With my forearms on my knees and my head bowed, I try to figure what to do. A couple breaths help to clear my mind. My head spins and my gaze sharpens as a small, barely heard noise comes from Eric. I'm out of time, unless I want to hit him again.

Boldly standing and walking up the stairs, I bring the gun to eye level and advance on the two men. They jerk and jump when they see me and reach for their weapons.

"Stop!" I yell. "Don't make me shoot you!"

Immediately, they stop reaching for their guns and put their hands up.

"Slowly! Slowly remove your weapons and throw them over here." They comply slowly when I sense a movement behind me. Stepping slightly to keep the men in my sights, I whirl toward the sound.

Adrien, having rolled out of his blankets, comes toward me at a run but slows as he nears.

"Ellen!" With deep breaths, Adrien halts beside me. His

features show fatigue but his eyes are intense.

"Adrien, where's Stephen?" I ask, turning fully back toward the men, scanning my gaze over the area.

"I don't know," he says, still confused with sleep. "He was here a few moments ago."

Nodding toward the men, I say, "Pat them down for guns and keys, Adrien. Anything you can find that we can use. Bring it here."

After checking for and finding keys on one man and phones on both, Adrien picks up the two guns on the ground and walks to my far side. Gesturing to the men to precede me, we move toward the pit in the middle of the courtyard.

"Get in," I say and give one of them a poke with the end of my gun barrel to get them moving. Gingerly, they step down the stairs, and I can tell the moment they see Eric by the expressions on their faces. Stepping slowly, they throw looks of shock and worry back to me.

"Now what, Ellen?" Adrien asks, but I don't know what to do. I'm totally winging this and give a small shrug and shake of my head.

"Ellen!"

Swinging quickly at the sound of my name, I level the gun at Stephen. He strolls down the stairs from the main building and has a large, welcoming smile on his face, his arms out wide. He looks totally put together, like he just had a shower. With his clean suit and neatly brushed hair he doesn't fit in with the rest of us. Adrien drops back and moves a bit to the side as he continues to cover the men in the pit.

Clasping his hands together in front of him, Stephen says, "There you are. I was wondering when you would be returning from down there." He makes a fluttering motion with his hand toward the pit. "And have you brought back my prize?"

Ignoring his question and nodding toward the pit, I say, "You're going to have to get in the hole with your men, Stephen."

"Don't be ridiculous. I'm not going anywhere — except with you, to our next location."

"That's not happening." I step back from him as he continues to advance toward me. "I don't want to shoot you. Be a good boy and get in the pit."

Stephen throws his head back and laughs at me. "Oh, Ellen. You won't shoot me. You just don't have it in you." His face changes and his eyes harden as he continues to stride toward me.

Suddenly, there's a loud shot. Stephen and I jump as a bullet ricochets off the ground right in front of him.

"She may not, Stephen, but I will take immeasurable pleasure in shooting you. *S'il vous plait*, do me a favor and continue to disobey. I'd love to have a reason to put a bullet in you."

Looking from Adrien to Stephen and back again, I realize he's serious. Do they have a history I'm unaware of? What the hell happened while I was underground?

Stephen's eyes jump quickly between Adrien and me, and it's obvious he believes Adrien will shoot him. Putting his hands up in a pacifying motion, he steps to the stairway and starts down.

"I don't know what good you think this will do you." He's talking to me but I barely hear; I'm done listening to him. "I'll follow you wherever you go. I'll find you."

"I believe you will. Or at least you'll try." Stepping from

him and the pit, I move backward toward the tree in the middle of the courtyard. "I'd better ensure a good head start, huh?" Saying that, I reach into the pot on the tree and remove the gold weight. With its removal, the ground gives a screech, and with a rotating motion the hole begins to close. Adrien and I stand and watch, listening the whole time as Stephen screams my name.

When the earth quits moving and we can no longer hear Stephen, I turn toward Adrien. I know there must be a dazed look in my eyes; I feel dazed. He grabs me tightly and gives me a hug, then holds me at arm's length and with a huge smile, looks me over.

"Oh, Ellen. I didn't know if I would ever see you again."

"I didn't know if you would either. It was touch and go for a while." With his hand lightly on the small of my back, we turn away from the courtyard and head toward the stairs into the building. "Do you have any water? How long was I gone?"

"This is the third morning since you left." As we mount the stairs, Adrien hurries forward and pulls a bottle of water from a container. Opening it and handing it to me, he says, "Slowly, my dear. Sip it first so you don't become ill."

I want to guzzle the water and find more and guzzle that too, but he's correct. I sip the water and ask, "Are there other supplies? We'll need everything they have, and a vehicle. I have Eric's keys and you have the others. One of the trucks must go to one of these keys. Let's grab the water and anything else in here and go."

We make three trips from the building to the vehicles; the whole time, I'm drinking water and feeling better—less lightheaded, though I could eat a horse. Adrien has questions for me, but I've asked him to give me time to process everything and to allow us to be on our way.

We try the vehicles and the keys work with two of them. There's no way to syphon gas from one vehicle to another, so we choose the one with the fullest tank. We move everything into it, including our belongings, which are in the back of the vehicle I arrived in. Stephen was telling the truth. When I take my bag out and dig into it, I pull the little box from the bottom. With a deep breath and a small prayer, I open it, and shining at me is the gold leaf. My face stretches in a huge smile as I look at Adrien. He's smiling and nodding at me, and I'm beginning to feel as if it might all be okay. Carefully, I place the gold weight in one of the box compartments.

"Ellen." Adrien's voice has a soft quality in the fading light of day.

"What is it, Adrien?"

"Did you find anything in the earth? What did you come back with?"

Untucking a portion of my shirt, I pull out the item taken from the reed basket. As I hold it up to show him, Adrien questions it. "A tarot card?"

"Yes," I say, turning it to take a good look at it. "The Wheel of Fortune."

"In the past, the Wheel of Fortune tarot card has been linked with the swastika based on the wheel and spokes. Other than that, I'm sorry, Ellen." His tone is crestfallen, and I glance at him. "I've been able to give you direction until now, but I have no idea what this means or where we are to go." He seems confused and disappointed. "And the words? Have any more come to you?"

"Yes." Moving closer to him, I give it a moment of thought. "You remember the words from the kachina, right? And the answer to them was 'faith.'"

"Yes, of course. Your famous leap of faith," he says with a small smile.

"Yeah. Cold water. So that was the first. Then, at the Buddha I was given another set of ..." With a shake of my head, a word comes to mind, and I shrug. "...clues. I guess what they are is clues. Anyway, at the Buddha, when I grasped the gold weight, I heard, 'Like spokes of a wheel, the skills are set. Truth and honesty are swept aside. Search deep and triumph well'..." Adrien doesn't ask any more questions, simply listens and lets me bounce ideas around. Really hear it all out loud for the first time and lay it out.

"Well, I came to realize what I needed to use was my imagination. To be cunning and utilize trickery." When I look up at him, he's nodding his head, understanding and urging me to continue.

"Then when I had the tarot card in hand, I heard, 'Time rolls on, turns evermore. Acceptance is approval, denial — rejection, to embrace the chance, to glimpse through the veil.'"

He stares at me and doesn't say anything for a few moments. "Can you tell me what you have deciphered? What, if anything, does this tell you?"

"I can and will, but let's head out. We'll talk about it in the vehicle, okay? I think we should stay on the move. Do you have any idea which direction we should head? Anywhere we'll be safe?"

With a nod and a far-off look, he says, "Yes. That I can help us with."

Soon we have everything we've found loaded into the

vehicle, and we head out. Adrien drives and I sip another bottle of water. I find a granola bar in the glove compartment and consume it as if it's filet mignon.

"Where are we going?" I ask him between bites.

"We're heading into Sekondi-Takoradi. There is a sea port, and I have a contact."

"Okay. What does that mean for us?"

"If one of his ships is in port, we'll be able to catch a ride. The odds of it taking us where we want to be are not great, but at least we will be out of here."

"That sounds good; that sounds very good." I want to discuss our situation, what's known, and what may come to be, but with the water and bar in my system, I'm drifting off. He's talking, and the cadence of his voice with the motion of the vehicle soon has me fast asleep.

Chapter 8

We've been at sea for three days. When we arrived at the Takoradi Harbour, Lady Luck was with us. Showing up unexpected at a foreign port, I didn't know what to think, but Adrien had it all under control. When we pulled up to the main building, he was greeted warmly with a hug and a handshake from a very big, very black man named Samuel. Samuel's attitude was jovial, and he seemed sincerely glad to see Adrien. When he glanced my way, I stepped to him and put my hand out.

"Samuel. It's nice to meet you."

Apparently, this wasn't the norm for him. He marched

right to me and wrapped me in a large hug. My body stiffened and my eyes bulged. Not used to being touched by strangers, I would normally keep people at arm's distance.

"Adrien, my old friend," he stated, making me wince with his booming voice next to my ear. "What have you been up to that you are traveling with such a lovely lady?"

"No, no, Samuel," Adrien replied with a shake of his head and a smile. "This is my good friend Ellen. If you have a moment, may we speak privately?"

"Of course. Come, come into my abode. We will sit and visit like civilized men." Saying that, he turned with me still under one arm and walked us into the building. Side-stepping a bit, I glanced over my shoulder at Adrien, a bit thrown off by Samuel and his manhandling. Adrien simply gestured with his hand to go as he followed.

Samuel's office was comfortable but cluttered. Paperwork—shipping manifests, service contracts, and maintenance documentation—among other items, were scattered everywhere. I didn't presume to understand how he could stay organized. He moved into the room ahead of us and swept papers off a set of armless chairs to drop them on a table by one wall.

"Sit! Sit and we will talk," he said, indicating the recently emptied seating. "A drink! We need a drink." He strode around his desk and with a thump and a squeak of protest from his chair, he sat and pulled open a drawer, withdrawing a bottle of bourbon and three small glasses. I looked at Adrien with a sideways glance and noted a barely perceivable nod in my direction. A drink we would have. Samuel, somehow graceful for a man of his size, poured the three glasses almost full of the deep-brown, amber liquid and handed them out, first to me and then to Adrien.

"To old friends!" he said in his thunderous voice and, saluting us, downed the contents in one gulp. "Ah!" he breathed out like a dragon and refilled his glass.

I smiled at his exuberant personality. Here was a person I couldn't help but like. Sitting back into the comfortable chair, relaxing for the first time in hours, I took a small sip from my glass. "Wow!" I uttered with a gasp and a cough, my eyes instantly watering.

"Ha, ha! Good stuff, eh?" Smiling, Samuel looked to Adrien. "So. What is it I can do for you?"

"Samuel," Adrien began and sat forward on the edge of his chair. "We require transportation. I am hoping we might look to you to help us with that," he said with a raise of his eyebrows.

Samuel sat back in his chair, and with an intent look at Adrien, he downed another shot of liquor. After the briefest of moments, he leaned forward and refilled his glass. Linking his hands, he glanced from Adrien to me and said, "Old friend…what have you gotten yourself into this time?"

"I am afraid I cannot divulge the nature of our predicament, much as I would like to confide in you. You will be safer if you don't know the particulars and if, once we are gone, you forget having seen us at all."

Samuel nodded his head in understanding and agreement. Tossing back another drink, he relaxed into his chair amid a burst of screeching. "All right. I have a ship leaving port tonight. It is bound for London. I can see you safely aboard."

"Yes, Samuel." Adrien nodded in return and, taking the shot of liquid fire, spoke in a weak voice with tears in his eyes.

"That would be wonderful."

So, under the cover of darkness, Adrien and I boarded a cargo ship bound for London, England.

The captain is polite but not friendly, and the crew — what I've seen of it — is hard working. It will take five days to reach London, and between here and there we have some decisions to make.

*****

I've been tossing around the idea of the tarot card from the tunnels and the clue I was given. When we got on the ship, we were put into a set of private quarters to share. It was only then I was finally able to really look the card over.

Pulling it from my belongings, I turn it this way and that in the faded light of the room. Something unnoticed before is the presence of faint symbols on the back side. With a firm rub of my thumb, I decide they don't seem to be written with ink or some other substance. They appear to be within the creation of the card. Now, not only is there the front side, which is fraught with symbolism to decipher for our uses, but there's also the symbols on the reverse. Adrien watches me study the card, so I hand it to him to get his impression.

"I'm sorry, Ellen," he says, turning it over with a passing glance and handing it back. "I do not have knowledge about tarot except, as I said, I have heard the link to the swastika and the Wheel of Fortune card."

"It's funny, in a weird way, to have one of the items we've found to be a tarot card." My elbows braced on my legs, I look at the card, turning it over and back. Tapping the edge of the card on my hand, letting my memory drift, I explain to Adrien. "When I was about twelve, I became fascinated by tarot. Two friends and I played around with it for a couple of years and then, as children do, we drifted apart from each other and from our enthusiasm with the cards and what we thought of as fortune telling."

"Your parents were indulgent of your learning about tarot?"

"Looking back, I realize, my parents were indulgent of anything I was curious about. Tarot, astronomy, mythology...many different subjects piqued my interest in those days. The stories of the world are fascinating. Little did I know those stories would lead me on this adventure to find the Guardian."

Nodding, as if he agreed and would expect this indulgence of them toward me, he asked, "Do you have any ideas about this card?"

Shaking my head, I rise to pace in our small space. "Not off-hand. There're so many possibilities. Astronomy, numerology, religion, mythology... I'm not sure where to go with it. And the symbols on the back. This," I say, pointing to one and leaning over him, "is like a stylized number four or something. It's peculiar, too..." I drift off, gazing at the ceiling. "It seems familiar, like I should remember...and this one? It's a sun cross." Shaking my head again, I see Adrien has that intense look back on his face. "What?"

"The sun cross is another representation of the swastika."

"Hmm—round and round we go."

"Ellen..."

At my name, I glance at Adrien again in question. He

stares at me but then drops his eyes.

"What is it, Adrien?"

Catching my eyes again, he asks, "Can you tell me about your experiences in the tunnels of Africa? What did you find there? How did you come by this tarot card? And what are your thoughts about the verse...the clue you have received?" He gestures in the direction of the card lying on my cot.

"I'm almost afraid to say anything—afraid you'll think me mad."

"With all we have already been through, you should know I do not discredit anything. What happened? What did you see?" He scoots eagerly to the edge of the cot, and with a resigned sigh, I join him.

"Did I ever tell you I have this weird fascination with spiders?"

Over the next hour, I tell Adrien about my adventure in the tunnels. I hesitate briefly before telling him of the large spider and almost don't tell him of the too-human face that looked out at me from that furry body.

"Ah, I understand now," he says with a nod of his head.

"What? What do you understand?" Scooting closer, I peer at him with a heightened awareness. What could he possibly know about this?

"There is an old folktale about a man-spider named Anansi who is the son of the Akan god, Nyame. This son is a conniver—a deceiver—and tales are told to children of him. They are tales of how Anansi outwits his friends, and often steals food for himself. He is thought to be very sly and funny."

"A conniver? A deceiver?" I say, repeating the terms

Adrien used. In my mind, I'm again seeing the face of the creature as I stood in the doorway with the card. He seemed so pleased, so proud. "Perhaps that's why it was required to use cunning on him."

"So how do you think this information, these experiences, will aid you in finding the Guardian? Where is this all leading you?"

With a weary shake of my head, I say, "I don't have any answers for you. The best I can do is understand the part of the prophecy these visitations are fulfilling. This Anansi is a folk tale. Old lore, right? The prophecy talks about stories from the past, the elders being seen as helping spirits. That's what this is all about. Where our stories come from, what they mean."

"Yes, you are correct. The prophecy says, 'Tradition and lore are inspired, through stories told from the past. The elders seen as spirits, as helpful aides they have been cast.' These spirits or elders must be leading you toward the new Guardian. They know you are the Key." He gives me a tired but optimistic smile and reaches to me to lay his hand gently on my shoulder. "This is good, Ellen. Your path is being set."

My mind flies in several directions, and I can't concentrate on one. I'm burning out and my brain is so tired. Sleep—I need to sleep and not have to think about any of it anymore. I want to let this settle and see what, if anything, my subconscious can come up with. "I need to sleep, Adrien. If it's all right with you, can we talk more in the morning?"

Adrien nods and, sliding down into his bunk, turns off the light.

*****

Standing on the bow of the cargo ship, I peer into the darkness, deep in thought. The night is crystalline. Looking into the pitch, it's impossible to see where the water ends and the sky begins—it's black on black, and the blanket of stars reflects in the liquid. Far under the deck the engines thump as they propel us through the water. It's a drum, felt as much as heard, vibrating up through the metal of the vessel and into my body. I'm on a space ship flying through eternity. *What a pleasure it would be to soar through galaxies without a care.*

Now, I stand on the ship looking out into infinity, my mind awash with questions. I'm daydreaming—or is it night dreaming? My thoughts wander, and the longer I stand, the closer the stars appear; we are becoming one. The lack of other stimuli confuses my brain. Is this an optical illusion or something? I'm being pulled into the night. Like a wash of warm water, sensations move from the crown of my head, flowing down. My buzz has gotten so commonplace, I hardly register it anymore.

In the far distance, one of the stars sparkles and flares, bright as a flashlight. My gaze is drawn to its brilliance. I'm captivated, entranced, as it grows larger, nearer—or am I moving toward it? No longer can I feel the thump of the engines or hear the splash of water on the hull of the ship; the world is absolutely silent. I'm spellbound by the radiance of the advancing orb. My eyes grow bigger and bigger, and my head tips back the closer we get to each other—as if I'm opening to take it in. The sphere begins to alter as it nears me. Its brilliance lessens but its features become more distinct. Soon it fills my vision—a huge, swirling, gaseous mass of red, brown, and a creamy off-white. The colors blend into horizontal lines, the only distortion a circle on the lower quadrant. *Of course,* I think. *I knew I recognized that symbol.*

"Ellen."

Adrien says my name, and just that quick I'm back in my body standing on the bow of the ship. I blink as the lap of the water sounds in my ears and vibrations from the engines move up my limbs from the depths. With a shaking hand, I reach to grasp the cargo next to me as I wobble slightly in my boots.

"You shouldn't be here alone," he chastises me gently. "It may not be safe."

"Thank you, Adrien." I turn to him and, seeing his silhouette in the darkness, reach to grasp his arm, giving it a small squeeze.

"Whatever for, *ma chère?*" His face is gentle in the dim light and his accent soothes my senses. I'm glad he's here with me, to keep me grounded.

"For being with me. For caring." Impulsively, I give him a hug.

With a gentle pat on my back, he mutters, "Of course, my dear. Of course." When I pull back from the hug, he takes my hand and tucks it under his arm. He turns me and begins to walk toward our quarters. "We'll be in London in a few days."

My mind, never still, jumps from his comment to a thought I've been avoiding. "Do you think they're dead? That I killed them?"

The quick change of subject throws him off, and he stops his forward motion. "Who?"

Standing beside him, I interlock my arms across my body, as if with a sudden chill. I peer down at my boots, then out into the ocean, not meeting his eyes. "The men in Africa. Maybe I shouldn't have put them into the hole. I've killed them." My voice cracks when the image of them dead in the tunnel springs into my mind.

"Did I ever tell you the story of the first time I met Stephen?"

Shifting to face him in the semi-darkness, I cock my head. "I knew it! I knew there was a history between you two." As I'm sure he's meant to, he's distracted me from my worry.

"Yes. When I first meet Stephen it was years ago, when your parents and I first became involved with the Guild and were still idealistic. I was somewhere I wasn't supposed to be, having accidently taken a wrong turn, and ended up in an elevator with a group of doctors. When the group exited, I followed. I still wake in a sweat over what I saw that day." Taking his hand in mine, I realize how cold he's become. "I tell you this so you will understand how truly evil Stephen is. You must be wary of him, Ellen."

"I understand, Adrien. He's crazy. I'm sure of that, just from the time I've had to spend in his company."

"No." His loose hand flails out to grasp both of mine, and with a desperate intensity he pulls me to face him. "Listen to me," he whispers. "When the group arrived in that room, it was where the children were kept. Children whom the Guild thought showed promise of developing into the Key. They were testing them...pushing their abilities to force a breakthrough." He drops my hands and turns from me as if ashamed or afraid to look me in the face. "Many nights, I still hear their cries."

"What happened?" I reach out and place a gentle hand

on his shoulder. "How did you get out of there?"

"The group was large enough that when they moved into an interior room of the lab, I was able to back out the door. No one even noticed when I got on the elevator. I went directly to your parents, and that very night we left." With his head down and staring at his feet, Adrien moves toward our cabin. A few moments later, he turns partially toward me and with an attempt to lighten the mood, says, "It's true, Stephen and I have had a run in or two in our time, and if there is one thing you can be assured of, he will always return—like a fungus."

I smile at him and allow him to ease the subject. With a grin, I respond to his pursed lips and the disgusted look on his face. "A fungus? Really, Adrien?" With a little chuckle, I take his arm and we resume our stroll toward our cabin. "So, you think they're okay?"

"Yes, my dear." His expression turns thoughtful and he pats my hand. "Unfortunately, I whole-heartedly believe we will have to deal with Stephen yet again."

I nod my head in understanding but am yet still unable to come to terms with the pull of different emotions—I hope they're alive, and I wish they'd leave us alone.

With a deep sigh, I state, "Rome."

"What did you say, Ellen?"

We walk slowly along as he stares at me. "Rome. Our next stop is Rome."

*****

Two days later, our ship docks at the Port of London.

I've been to London before in my travels for work, but

I've never entered her shores from the port. The city of London lies on the River Thames and is full of the hustle and bustle of a major metropolis. It's hard to fathom, but London is bigger than New York City. In population, they're comparable, but in land mass London is double the size. I wish we could spend some time here; I love London. But we know if we dawdle it may be the downfall of everything we've gained. We quickly disembark from the ship without seeing the captain, who has been mostly absent from our vicinity. Hefting our bags, we walk to the nearest street, hoping to catch a taxi. We'll head straight to Heathrow Airport; a cab ride will take about an hour and a half.

In the taxi, the city passes, and I chance an occasional glance at Adrien, unable to help but wonder at his thoughts. When I told him our next destination was Rome, he couldn't quit firing off questions.

It was hard—complex—to explain to him why Rome. How did I know, with such certainty, Rome was it? How do I explain the vision of Jupiter that came to me? The fact that Jupiter is linked with the Wheel of Fortune card, and Jupiter is Roman? One of the symbols on the reverse side of the card, the abstract number four, is the symbol for Jupiter. I finally had to shake my head at him and ask him to give me some of that trust and faith he's asked from me. I can't explain it fully to him, but we need to go to Rome and so to Rome we will go.

For the last two days, every time we were together or passed each other on the ship, he would look at me with his eyes full of questions, but at least he quit asking them. I already have an idea of where we need to go when we arrive in Italy. My certainty extends to what the other symbols on the back side of the card mean — what the card itself means — but I haven't told Adrien yet; I'll let his mind work on the link to Rome.

*****

Sitting on the plane, waiting for takeoff, Adrien leafs through a magazine and appears relaxed. He's come to terms with our destination, even without answers. We boarded easily enough after I got rid of the guns in the ladies' room garbage. Sad, but necessary. Luckily, our passports and cash were with the rest of our things in the back of the vehicle.

"Tell me something you remember about my parents," I prompt him.

His attention drawn from the magazine, he closes it gently and leans forward to put it back in the seat pocket. Softly, he speaks to me. "I believe the traits that most stand out when I think of your parents were their strong sense of right and wrong and their character. They were the smartest, most driven people I've ever met. You are an amazing combination of them. You have their intelligence and wit and your own brand of cunning." He reaches to take my hand in his and looks me in the eye. "Watching as you grew, I felt as proud of you as if you were my own." He releases my hand, pats it, and leans back in his chair when the plane begins to taxi down the runway. We're both silent as the sun spikes through the windows and we soon leave the earth to head toward Italy.

When the plane levels out, he speaks again. Conversation picks up around us and I lean toward him to make certain I hear every word.

"The day I met your parents, as I told you, we attended a reading by an author who interested us. He discussed a book he'd written on the origins of the world's folklore—ancient texts and images that have been found around the world. Funny how such a subject can bring like-minded individuals together. The reading was interesting and the author also, but the true catalyst for our relationship was a woman we met there. Lila was part of a larger group, an ancient sect, which for generations had followed the prophecy—waiting for the coming of the Key. She was charismatic. One of those people who naturally drew others to her."

I'm held by his words. Finally, information on my parents and their part in this portion of my life.

"The subject of the prophecy was something your parents and I gravitated to, questioned. The idea of other beings, beings who watch over us, elders who have been there from time untold, resonated with us. All our history and ancient tales ultimately being tracked back to them. How interesting. How wonderful.

"We were captivated. Ripe for the picking and ready to be manipulated by an unethical woman. As I look back, I see we were as children running out of control down a hill—not aware of or caring for dangers that may lie at the bottom. When it became obvious her infatuation for your mother, due to her pregnancy, was unnatural, the three of us broke from her and her followers. We never imagined her interest in the discovery of the Key might harm living beings—ourselves and you among them—but soon it was too obvious to deny.

"Before my experience in the lab, we'd heard talk, initially only rumors, of children being gathered. Children with a tendency toward certain psychic abilities. Our fear was that Lila wanted you, and after what I saw and my telling of it to your parents, we knew this wasn't where we wanted to be. That was when your parents moved back to America. In France, I kept my ears and eyes open for any information about her, and your parents were vigilant in your care and safety. None of us ever saw this woman again."

"But, Adrien," I interrupt him to ask. "Are Stephen and his men part of it, part of this Guild? Is that why they showed up and won't leave us alone?"

Adrien directs a piercing look at me for a moment, a look full of fear and determination, and then with a shake of his head, he reaches to take my hand in his. "Stephen is a very bad man. He's cut from the same cloth as Lila, but he's much, much worse. She dreamed and hoped, perhaps acted unethically, but he truly believes he will be the one to control not only the Key, but the Guardian as well."

"How can he think that? I mean, what would that even mean? Control of a supreme being? How delusional is he?"

Adrien gives a small snort of a laugh. "Oh, Ellen. He's highly delusional. He thinks himself to be the next God. He just needs to position himself on the top layer of the universal food chain, and that is something we must never allow. The world as we know it would cease to exist."

I scoot forward in my seat, so intent on the conversation, I'm leaning into him. "So why don't I just walk away? If the Guardian is never found, Stephen can never attempt to take control of him, right? The group has waited eons for the Key to come, and if I quit, it's feasible they'll have to wait for eons more. By then, Stephen will be long dead."

"I don't think you can just walk away, Ellen. The game is in motion, the Key in play. We're going to need to see this out until the end—no matter what. We must be diligent and not allow Stephen to take control. Not of you, and not of the Guardian."

Sitting straight and leaning back into my seat, I wonder, *how can I ensure that?*

As we land in Italy, I'm reminded of another time I was in this country. I was on a quest of sorts then, too, on my way to Naples looking for a treasure. This time it's Rome. Rome and the Sanctuary of Fortuna.

Chapter 9

The Sanctuary of Fortuna Primigenia at Palestrina.
Beautiful.

Standing before the temple of rock, I'm in awe at what humans can create. The sanctuary rises above me in five stone tiers, each one built upon the other. In my life, I've been privileged to behold many amazing achievements of mankind, but what continues to astound me is the age, the timeless antiquity of these structures. They echo with voices from eons past. Their very scent is of the earth: ancient, old, and wise.

Speaking to Adrien, I say, "Where do you think we

should start?"

Staring up at the rock formation, Adrien is silent. With a small glance in my direction, his eyes give away his thoughts on the immense task ahead of us. He heaves a heavy breath and drops his gaze to ground level. "From the bottom up, I propose."

"Sounds like a valid plan." This comes out with forced cheerfulness. When he raises his eyebrows at me, I give him a small smirk and pat his shoulder. Resigned, we start forward.

The bottom tiers are sided by wide stairs and covered in a grassy plane. They're the base for the more intricate parts of the temple, and require some hiking. After reaching the summit of the second level, I pause to catch my breath. The higher we climb, the more of the city is revealed to our gazes. It unfolds like a blossom in the morning light.

To reach the next terrace, we utilize one of two side ramps. This terrace sits at the top of two blind arches that are built one atop the other. Past this point, we climb the central stairs to the fourth and fifth levels. Each of the five levels are open to the sky. They are grass-covered, and when I turn around to catch my breath, it stops in my throat. From this height, I can see for miles.

"Oh, Adrien. Isn't the view fantastic?" I'm breathless, and it isn't all from the climb. The town of Palestrina lies out before us like a technicolor map. All the buildings, houses, and businesses are made of the same stone and have red tile roofs. In the distance, we see the open land of the hillside. The clarity and crispness of the air makes everything stand out in stark relief. The contrast of colors—mustard yellow of the buildings, red of the roof tiles, greens and purples of the hills—it's like a master's painting.

Standing beside me, Adrien leans forward and places his hands on his thighs. He's taking deep breaths. Sometimes, it's easy to forget he's significantly older than me and lives a sedentary life. I watch him for a moment out of the corner of my eye and then take his arm to turn him toward the stairs.

"Let's sit for a sec and let me catch my breath, shall we?"

He easily sees through my charade to give him some rest, but to give him credit, he doesn't argue. As we sit, enjoy the view, and sip our bottled water, Adrien returns to the topic of where we are.

"This shrine—you said it was built to honor a major goddess?"

"Yes, Fortuna was a Roman goddess of fortune—both good and bad. She fits right into our scope of ideas, as she's often shown with a wheel of fortune or balanced scales. She's the oldest daughter of the Roman god Jupiter, and that symbol on the tarot card, the intricate number four—that's the symbol for Jupiter."

Adrien listens intently. This is the first time I've explained to him what train of ideas brought us here.

"This sanctuary is one of the oldest and largest of her temples in Italy, so I figured it was a good place to start."

"Do you have any thoughts of what we search for?"

"Absolutely none," I say with conviction, but still I am certain we're in the right place. Where this certainty comes from, I don't know. But it's deep in my bones. At this point, it doesn't matter if I don't understand. I'm willing to go with the flow and see where it leads me.

Adrien stands and turns toward the main hall of the sanctuary. "I'm rested well enough, Ellen. Are you ready to proceed?"

"Yes," I state and rise to my feet. "Let's proceed."

We climb the staircase to the main hall.

As we ascend the stairs, we view more and more of the upper tier. In the center of the terrace is an alcove with a weathered stone statue — Fortuna, I presume. The statue is still recognizable as female, shrouded in a tunic-style dress, but her face is so weathered her features are long gone. Still, she's beautiful. She speaks of the ages that have passed, the days she's seen come and go. Directly above and behind her, on the final terrace, is the sacred well with a theater, its seats wrapped in a half-circle. Behind the theater is a three-story building with many windows, built in a mirror image of the theater.

Adrien moves up the final staircase, but I can't pull myself from the statue. I stare at her, transfixed. *Speak to me, Fortuna. What would you tell me if you could?*

"Ellen!" Adrien calls and breaks the invisible bonds keeping me in place.

"Yes?" With a step back, I look up the stairs but can't see him, I only hear his words calling down.

"Come look at the well. There are images, figures engraved in it. Perhaps this is what we are looking for."

With one final glance over my shoulder at the statue of Fortuna, I climb the stairs to stand beside Adrien. The well is aged, worn and indistinct like everything else here, but interesting. All around are panels with images of faces — gods, maybe? With a slow step, I pace around the well, walking in a circle, searching for meaning in the images, but nothing speaks to me. I touch the surface of the well. It's rough stone, warmed by the sun's heat. With a tilt of my body, I place my hands on the edge of the well and lean to peer into its depths.

Giving a shrill whistle, I listen to the sound quickly dissipate. Nothing, not even an echo. Just a well. *What now?*

"What do you think, Ellen?"

"I don't know," I look around, scanning the area. "I thought I'd feel directed, pulled somewhere. I don't feel anything."

We wander aimlessly, looking and touching everything. As time passes, the feeling of discouragement grows. We're unable to discover anything but history and rocks. My conviction is so great this is the place I need to be — *why won't it speak to me?*

The day flies as we scour every inch of the sanctuary. Five tiers of grand and deteriorating rocks. *Nothing.*

"It looks as if we will be spending the night," Adrien says from behind me as we stand at the foot of the shrine. We watch as the sunlight fades and then get into our rental to head to our hotel.

*****

The next day passes much as the first. We spend most of our time in the palace set atop the sanctuary. It was built by the Barberius, a ruling family, when they came into power. Situating their palace upon the five terraces of Fortuna's temple gave them an awe-inspiring view of the countryside.

The palace is built in a semi-circle around Fortuna's theater and well. Though it's not the size of most modern palaces, it's quite imposing and takes us most of the second day to search. *Still nothing.*

"Well, my dear," Adrien says, finally broaching the

subject, "it appears we'll be spending another evening at our lodgings."

I trudge to the steps of the theater and sit heavily, dropping my chin into my hands. I was so certain. *What am I missing?*

Adrien steps over to sit alongside me on the steps. The sun, in its last burst of life for the day, shines bright and a small breeze blows. The beauty of the evening is dampened by my disappointment.

With a hesitant glance in my direction, he adds, "Are you certain this is the correct location?"

"I was." Now, however, I'm not so sure. Where has my confidence gone?

"We will have to hunt out the location of the other temples erected to honor Fortuna. Perhaps we can break them down by size and region to formulate a…"

Adrien's voice drones on in regard to how we will continue our search, but I'm zoning out, allowing him to take the lead with the plans.

Like pushing through mud, a sound comes to me, or maybe it's a change in the air patterns — with my stare locked in the distance, I try to capture what's altered.

Is that someone humming?

The sound of Adrien's voice continues in the back of my mind, but my attention is honing in on the new sound. The humming. Singing?

The sound of it pulls me to my feet as if I'm a marionette on a string. As I move forward, I have a fleeting thought: this must be what sailors felt as the sirens sang to them. To be compelled; the urge is so intense — so sweet — even if I wanted to resist, I couldn't.

Behind me, Adrien continues on about other locations and my thoughts on solving our problem.

I can't concentrate on his words, and his voice is drowned out by the incessant pull of the humming.

There! There it is. Wafting on the breeze. A song; lovely.

I move forward, down the steps of the amphitheater, and as I pass the well, my fingertips run over the surface. It's warm and pulsates with a life that was missing so short a time ago. Should I be freaking out at the discovery that a stone well has a life presence? Maybe. Perhaps later I'll think about it. Right now, a back part of my mind fills with a pleased anticipation of something finally happening, and the greater part swirls in the cloud of humming. The fog of my mind becomes tangible as I move down the stairs and past the well; my vision is obscured as a mist rolls in. I inhale deeply, and it registers that this haze doesn't have the cool moisture of a mist; it's smoke, incense. The scent fills my head, and a dizziness overtakes me. I'm moving, walking down pathways and stairs, but to where, I don't know. Everything is shrouded in the vapor, hidden from my view as my footsteps echo hollowly and my feet move unerringly, taking me to my destination.

How long has it been? I'm not conscious of time but my body doesn't feel fatigue. I must have only traversed a short distance. Ahead of me the smoke thins, and I make out a man-made doorway, its stone arched and almost six feet tall. Through the archway and down a set of stairs, the temperature drops, and the aroma changes and sharpens. There's a chill on my skin. Outside, the sun was warm and welcoming, but here in the lowest level of the shrine, it's cool and moist.

In the interior, my footfalls strike the walls and echo back to me. It's dimly lit and hazy with only a small illumination from the brave rays of sunlight that push inside. I take a deep breath to corral my nerve to move farther inward. A torch flares on my left, startling me back a step. Several feet of dirt floor are illuminated, and with slow strides, I move forward. Just as I reach the end of the light, another torch flares to life further in. The lighting torches lead me down a stone hall for several feet until the pathway opens into a small cave. In this grotto, there's candlelight all around, a beautiful mosaic makes up much of the floor, and the sound of a bubbling fountain catches my attention.

Craning my neck to see more, I'm surprised when a woman steps from behind the fountain. She's mesmerizing, dressed in a long, flowing tunic that reaches the floor. Her dress looks like a coarse material, perhaps wool, but it's a beautiful dark rose color. Her hair is intricately braided and wrapped about her head. Considering her face, I'm captivated by her gaze and barely register the fact she's old. Ancient. Her visage is timeworn and leathery, her gait slow and stooped. As she moves forward, she leaves scratch marks in the dirt floor from her shuffling, sandal-clad feet and the hem of her tunic.

When she appeared around the fountain, I stopped in my tracks, but as she nears me, her gaze pulls me in and I continue on to her. Her eyes reflect the light in the room and sparkle like gemstones. Blue? Green? I can't make out their true color, but they're intense. She's much more than the old lady she first appears.

I stop a step in front of her.

With a gentle reach, she touches my arm and utters,

"kóri."

Daughter.

How am I able to understand her? What language is she speaking?

She turns from me and, stepping back, gestures toward a wooden chest.

"Epiléxte."

Choose?

Clarity comes to my brain as the clue I was given at the taking of the tarot fills my head: *Time rolls on, turns evermore. Acceptance is approval, denial – rejection, to embrace the chance, to glimpse through the veil.*

I slide past her and with a stretch of my neck and a tip sideways, I peek into the case. In the flickering light, small panels of wood inlayed with symbols are visible. Letters? Are there letters on them?

Choose? One? More? And why?

With a glance back at her, I see she's watching me, waiting for me.

The answer to the clue enters my thoughts. Of course. Choice. To be willing to make a choice. Willing, with open eyes and a clear heart—no turning back.

I take a long look at the old woman, and the confusion and fear, that have been building over the past few days dissipates.

The choice is open to me. When I realize this, there's no force, no coercion. I'm able to make my own decision, forward or backward—it's mine to make. I will continue this quest. I will embrace my destiny as the Key, and I will discover the Guardian and see him to his place among the immortals.

With a quick step, I move beside the crate and squat. I

quit thinking and simply plunge my hand into the wooden tiles, grip as many as I can, and pull back. Standing and turning, I thrust my hand out at her and open my fist.

"*Na ríxei.*"

Throw.

Glancing down at the dirt floor, with a small toss, I scatter the tiles at our feet.

With a quick, bird-like movement, she drops and peers at the pieces, hovering her palm a few inches above each one, humming and swaying as if lightly buffeted by a breeze.

What is she looking for? What can she see? Can she sense something? Wonder enters my being, and I kneel beside her, watching every move she makes.

Selecting a tile, she holds it out to me and whispers, "*Drákon.*"

"Drago," I repeat, and am startled when my whisper sounds in another language. A language I don't know but somehow understand and now speak. But speaking isn't comprehension. What does she mean by "drago?"

With a selection of the second tile, she says, "*Naós póli.*"

Temple City?

What else can she tell me? What will I learn?

With the selection of the third and final tile, she moves closer to look me directly in the eye and states, "*Frourá.*"

"Guard."

Drago. Temple City. Guard.

"I don't know what you mean. What am I supposed to do?"

With a thin crooked finger, she reaches out and touches my forehead, causing everything to go dark.

*****

"Ellen... Ellen."

Faint sounds echo to me out of the distance. Low, causing a vibration through my system. With the hum of sounds comes the sensation of touch. Someone is beside me. Gently shaking me — a hand on my shoulder.

"Ellen. Are you all right, my dear?"

It's Adrien, his worried voice in my ear. His tender touch on my arm.

As I come back, a rush of smells assails me. Dirt, moisture, and that unique chalky scent of rock. I open my eyes to a scattered darkness and as my vision clears, my hands come into focus. They're on my lap, palms up, open. Within them are the tiles given to me by the oracle. I close my fists about them, and the words slice into my head:

Advance forward, ever changing, ever growing.
Fortitude is cast,
despair forsaken.

"Ellen. Shh... It's all right. You're all right."

After a moment to wonder what he's talking about, a splash hits my hand. I'm crying. Why am I crying?

With a deep, shuddering breath, I raise my head and catch Adrien's eye.

Our visibility of each other is limited, illuminated only by the small flashlight he carries. His face is in partial shadow, but the worry in his eyes is evident.

I'm sitting on my feet with my legs bent under me. I can tell I've been here awhile because my feet are tingly, and the cold from the floor has seeped into my bones. When I woke, my chin was on my chest and now my neck feels strained.

How long have I been here?

"Ah, my dear. There you are." Adrien slides down on the ground next to me and places an arm around my shoulders. He reaches into his jacket pocket and pulls out a handkerchief, handing it to me.

When I don't move, simply watch him, he wipes the tears from my cheeks.

"Adrien?"

"Yes, Ellen. Why are you crying?"

I shake my head at him. I remember the vision of the oracle. The words she said to me as she handed me each tile. And I remember more—I remember the vision she gave me with her touch. But I don't believe it; how can I believe it? I need to think.

I'm disoriented and my eyes are heavy, the flesh swollen. Looking up, I scan the area.

My body aches, but I shift the tiles into one hand and reach to take the flashlight from Adrien. With an outstretched arm and a quick glance, I pan the light around the room. There's a sense of recognition. It's the same, yet different. With the oracle, the cave was lit by candle and torch. The fountain had flowing water and a beautiful mosaic covered part of the floor. Now it is all gone; had it ever been? Or was it yet to be? In the dark, I can just make out what may be a base of the fountain. There's nothing but dirt on the floor.

My eyes meet Adrien's as he studies me.

"Can you help me to stand?"

He places his arm around my waist, and with my hand firmly grasping his shoulder as he stands, he pulls me up with him.

"Ah, hell." My legs are asleep, and it hurts to put my weight on my feet.

Uttering a small moan and keeping my eyes on the floor, I walk in a circle to get the circulation moving again in my feet and legs.

"What happened? What do you have?"

Ignoring his questions for the moment, I ask one of my own. "How long have you been here? What did you see?"

"You wandered away from the theater. I followed you until you arrived in this cave. You sat on the ground speaking some foreign language. I'm not sure, but I think it was Greek. I didn't know you spoke Greek."

"I don't."

With a raise of his eyebrows, Adrien meets my gaze.

"What do you have?" he asks again.

Unfolding my fingers, I open my hands and show him the tiles. He takes the flashlight back and shines the beam on them. We stand looking down, studying them. The only sound is a drip of some far-away water. What did the old woman mean by drago, temple city, and guard?

Light from the setting sun streaks in from the outside and draws me to it. The need to feel the sunshine—the warmth on my skin—is an irresistible urge. Adrien follows as I walk slowly toward the entrance of the cave and out into the luminous beauty of early evening.

Outside in the near dark, we again study the tiles. They each have symbols, some form of markings on them. They're like nothing I've ever seen before.

I peer at them. "What do you think?"

"I don't recognize the writing. Perhaps there is someone

in Palestrina who can translate the tiles."

"All right," I say, looking toward the lowering sun. It flares as it dies, causing me to squint. "It's getting pretty late, though. The shops are going to be closed and I need some rest. Let's ask around in the morning."

Chapter 10

The city of Palestrina is ancient. Timeless and beautiful like an elderly woman.

I've always enjoyed this type of city. Narrow avenues with cobblestone paths. The buildings are tall, two stories, and most of the upper stories have small balconies with flowers hanging from them. It's picturesque.

There are a variety of shops: coffee shops, tourist shops, and many others. Adrien and I stop in a few but are no closer to figuring out the tiles. No one seems to have any idea about what they say or what they mean. At the last shop, a young man recommends we speak with the owner of a coffee shop on the next street. In broken English, he informs us that Signor Romano knows many varied languages and may be of service.

When we walk into the coffee shop in question, simply named Café Italiano, we are greeted by a beautiful young woman. She is chicly dressed in skinny black jeans, leather boots, and a creamy sweater over a dark shirt.

"*Benvenuto!*"

"Good morning," I respond to her. "We're looking for Signor Romano. Do you know if he's available?"

"Oh, *sì. Sì.* He is my *nonno*…um…grandfather. *Un momento*, I will get him for you."

The young woman disappears into the back room, and a moment later, reappears with a small, elderly man. He's stooped and wrinkled and reminds me of an old potato.

"*Sì*," he says. "How may I help you?"

"Signor Romano. We were told you might be able to translate something for us. If we might have a moment of your time…privately?"

Mr. Romano stares at us for a moment, and I'm sure he's deciding if we are worth his time. With a small nod and a wave of his hand, he turns back toward the rear of the building. Adrien and I follow him with an air of hope and expectation.

The back room is a serviceable kitchen, and through another door seems to be a small office. Mr. Romano turns toward us and lifts one eyebrow. I guess that means "Get on with it."

Without preamble, I pull the tiles from my bag and lay them carefully on the counter.

"Signore, can you tell us what these tiles say?"

Picking up the tiles and turning them over, Mr. Romano

gives them a thorough inspection. He replaces them on the counter and looks first at Adrien and then at me.

"Where did you come by these?"

I stare at him but don't offer any explanation for the tiles. A burst of possessiveness explodes within me. I control it, tamp it down, and repeat my request.

"Can you tell us what they say?"

At first, I don't think he's going to be of any help. Looking at the tiles, he again picks each one up, studies it, and sets it gingerly back on the table. He exhales a mighty breath and shakes his head, still looking at the tiles. "I don't understand."

Resigned, I nod. "You can't tell us what they say." I reach for the tiles when he places his hand over them and looks me in the eye.

"No. I can tell you what they say, I just don't understand what they say."

Maybe there is some information to be gotten here. "You know, I get a lot of that. I'd appreciate anything you can tell us."

He picks up each tile, one after the other, and as he translates he hands them to me.

"This one loosely says, 'Above so below.'"

Something about that phrase sets off a pinging in my head. I tip my head back to stare at the ceiling, thinking. *Above so below...* Why does that sound so familiar?

Adrien steps closer and whispers, "On Earth as it is in heaven."

Startled by this comment, this link to something I know — a foundation of my life — I swing to stare at him. Is this a tie to another of man's stories? What's it all mean? Adrien doesn't volunteer anything else. I pivot back to watch Mr. Romano.

He studies the second tile and raises an eyebrow to look at me. His face is flushed and although his demeanor gives very little away, he seems to be excited. "You really must tell me how you acquired these tiles."

Now he has my curiosity all atwitter. Stepping closer to the table, I lean in to look down at the stone in his hand.

"What does it say?"

"It is the symbol for Vishnu."

"Vishnu? The god Vishnu?" I turn to look at Adrien again, including him in my question. "Is any of this making sense to you?"

He steps closer to the table. "Yes, somewhat. Vishnu is one of three main male deities of the Hindu faith."

"Heaven. Gods. Above so below. What does the third tile say?" I'm joining him in the feeling of excitement now. I don't know what it all means, but at least it's some information, something to work with.

"Consumer of evil." When he says these words, Mr. Romano appears confused. He hands me the final tile, steps back from the table, and gives me a look that seems to see straight through my skin and bones.

"I have someone who I think you should meet." After stating this, he waits. Does he think I'll say no? I need all the help I can get.

"All right. Who might that be?"

"She's a teacher. And a student — of the world."

Nodding slowly, I ask, "And how do I go about meeting this woman?"

"I'll call her — now. She, I think, will love to meet you."

About twenty minutes later, the front door bell jingles and I glance at Adrien. We've been waiting impatiently and my nerves are frayed. With the bell, my breathing quickens, and I swear the pressure in the room changes. Adrien stares back at me, but he doesn't seem to notice the change in atmosphere.

Through the curtain into the back room sweeps a woman. I stare at her, wide-eyed. She must be used to this reception wherever she goes. Her clothing is made from the loudest fabric I've ever seen, and due to the multitude of bangles on her wrists, she's brought her own brand of music with her. Although she looks to be in her late sixties, her hair is jet black. The messy coil of it bounces and threatens to fall with each step. No millimeter of naked skin can be found on her face and neck due to the plastering of pancake makeup sculpting over its hills and valleys. Her eyes are done in dark black kohl, and her lips, while ruby red, are drawn haphazardly on. She has rings on every finger and long, unsightly nails. She is a sight to behold.

"*You!*" she shouts as she advances. Adrien has dropped back along a wall, well out of sight. I can't help stepping back as she moves to within a few inches of me. Due to my height, I'm looking down at her, but she's imposing nonetheless.

"*You.* You are the one needing my assistance."

Dang! I'm not sure if that's an accurate statement or not. What could she have to offer?

"Um..."

With a step closer, the woman reaches out and gives me a thump on the chest. I move back again, completely shocked, only to come up against the edge of the table.

"Hey! Wait just a minute—"

"*No.* No minutes." With a pace away, she throws her head back, eyes squinted, and whispers, "Show me what you have."

Drama, much?

I must say, I'm skeptical of this woman. She's just so over the top. It's as if we're in a circus tent with Madam Zola or something. If I weren't so desperate, I'd take my tiles and leave. But who knows? Figuring nothing lost nothing gained, I place the three tiles on the table in front of us.

"Ah." She sways in a rhythmic motion over and back from the tiles. Her eyes are opened to just a slit, and she's humming lightly.

I scan the room. I'm a bit embarrassed, and for being here myself.

"You must go to the city. To the dragon."

At this, my attention is absolute. Dragon. That's what the oracle said. Something I haven't told anyone—not even Adrien. Maybe there's something to her after all.

"What city? What dragon?" I step nearer to where she sways, my head tilted, watching her intently.

"To Garuda."

I listen closely to her low voice, my brows wrinkled, leaning in. I hear her, but again I don't understand what she's saying. With a quick glance, I look at Adrien to see he appears as confused as I am. Mr. Romano doesn't offer any assistance.

City? Dragon? Garuda?

Suddenly, she blinks her eyes and the life returns to them.

"Tell me, quickly…tell me what was said."

I scan the room, looking to the two men to see who will volunteer an answer. When no one talks, I figure it must be me.

"You said 'city,' 'dragon,' and 'Garuda.'" I focus on the shop owner and then slide my eyes back to the woman. "Signor Romano told me the tiles say 'above so below,' 'Vishnu,' and…ah… 'Consumer of Evil.'"

"Ah. Yes, yes. One of the three. Of course…" She trails off, mumbling to herself as she paces the room.

I follow her with my eyes, avidly watching, waiting for an additional bit of information. I may have been skeptical about her at first, but I'm on board now.

"What do you mean, 'One of the three?' What did you see?"

She moves quickly to the bag she dropped upon entering the room and, reaching in with a flourish, pulls out a worn deck of cards. A tarot deck.

My body caves inward as a harsh breath leaves my lungs, and I can't seem to pull any air in. The only sound in the room is the beating of my heart. I concentrate, and with a desperation, I fill my lungs. In; out. In; out. *Just breathe, Ellen.*

A tarot deck. Why does she have a tarot deck?

Leafing through the deck, the woman pulls out a single card.

"One of the three," she says with a brandishing sweep of her arm and slaps the Wheel of Fortune card down in front of me. I stare at it, transfixed. What's the likelihood? Out of seventy-eight cards, what are the odds the Wheel of Fortune would come into play again? I glance toward my bag on the floor, expecting my card to be burning a hole in it.

"What do you mean?" My voice is a squeak. Clearing my throat, I try again. "What do you mean? How does this card help us?"

"Look at it." She's leaning over and practically stroking the card. "It's beautiful. All the symbols. All the imagery. Everything you need to know is clear on the card."

I nod my head at her. This all makes sense, except I don't know how to read the card.

"Will you tell me? Will you read the card for me?"

"One of the three. The symbols on the card give us direction." Touching the card with a finger topped by a long, yellow nail, she indicates the figure sitting on the top of the wheel. "The Sphinx." With a shift, she moves her finger to the red figure hanging on the right side. "The pyramids." Finally, she looks to where she's stroking the card and my eyes follow her hand. The image of the snake on the left side of the wheel. Again and again her finger plays over the serpent.

"Drago. One of the three."

"Yes, I see. The snake."

"*No*. The dragon."

"Okay, okay, the dragon. What is represented by the dragon image?"

She looks from her finger moving on the card up into my eyes, and the smile that grows on her face has me itching to step back. Her eyes glaze and then roll part way back into their sockets. She was freaky before, but with her inward glance, chills run from my nape down my spine.

Her voice is monotone and droning. "Yes. Yes, your travels are determined by a fate not your own. You must journey to the Temple City. You must find the amulet and be burnt by Garuda. Only then will the Key move forward and find the Guardian…"

I make a grab for her as she slumps, almost falling to the floor. Adrien and Mr. Romano rush forward, and we clamber around her, maneuvering her into a chair. Each of us with a lost look, not knowing what to do. Squatting next to the chair, I gently push her back, tipping her head so I can see into her face. She's unconscious, her breath deep and even.

Mr. Romano comes around the front of the table with a cup of steaming tea, but seeing she's not conscious, he sets it on the table.

The men and I share a look. Blank stares, each of us feeling inept in our attempts to help the woman. She seems comfortable enough, so leveling my gaze at the shop keeper, I say, "The Temple City. Do you know what or where that is?" In my head, all I hear is the oracle using the same words — Temple City.

"Yes. Come, I will show you." He walks away from us, heading farther into the room. I glance at Adrien and stand.

"Stay with her, Adrien."

This day keeps getting weirder and weirder. I follow him to the back wall where he stops at a large book of maps. Using his entire body to maneuver the book, he flips several pages open until he comes to one that shows Asia. The southeast corner of Asia. He reaches out a gnarled finger and taps Cambodia.

"There. The Temple City — Angkor Wat. It is there you must go."

Chapter 11

The sun shines hot on our heads. Even covered by a hat, it bakes into my skin and blinds my eyes. There's a whole different intensity to the quality of sunshine in Cambodia. Its heat is only eclipsed by its brilliance. I'm thankful for my sunglasses, though even with them on, the light creates occasional blind spots when reflected on certain surfaces. The foliage is dense where it hasn't been cleared by men, and even where it has, I'm able to see the jungle striving to take back its land. The tangled forest will be here long after humans are gone from this earth. It's obvious the retaking will be done with ease.

Angkor Wat. Temple City.

What will we find here? What did the woman mean by "You must be burnt by Garuda?"

Getting to and into Cambodia didn't present much of a problem. A visa was required, but with Adrien's contacts, we managed that easily. We flew into Siem Reap International Airport, and from there, the temple complex of Angkor Wat was only three miles away. If it wasn't so hot and humid, I'd have loved to walk the distance.

After we landed and went to a hotel, we made a quick trip to a shopping center. In this climate, there's a list of items one would want to carry. My bag is now stuffed with provisions such as sun screen, lip balm, insect repellent, a rolled-up poncho, and a small flashlight. Adrien and I are sporting new hats and sunglasses.

I had assumed we were going to have a relatively easy go of it and the searching of another temple, but then we arrived and I got a look at a map of the Angkor Archaeological Park. The park covers more than 400 square kilometers and houses fifty temples. We may be here for a while.

Adrien and I stroll along the grass paths, staying vigilant for any changes in the nuance of Angkor Wat. As is usual, we don't know what we need — don't even know what to look for, but this time I have a feeling of doom. There's a quality of dread, and my animal instincts are bristling. My breathing is a bit faster, my hearing more acute. My eyes shift endlessly from one object or building to another, ready for something unidentifiable. On the surface, it seems a perfectly normal day—birds call in their many different languages and a myriad of insects sing to one another, their buzzes, chirps, and clicks at times so deafening I find myself glancing around in alarm, as if expecting a scourge of creepy crawlers to be advancing on us, ready for a meal. I'm reminded of the feelings of panic from the African tunnels and the sensation of disgust when confronted by the huge spider.

The oppressive heat is an entity wearing us down. It's a force that alters the earth's gravity, causing me to strain to walk and even breath. The air is heavy, thick. It's difficult to draw it into my lungs and almost impossible to push it out again. I have rivers of sweat running down my spine and between my breasts. Every moment or two, Adrien wipes his face and neck with his handkerchief. We are ill-equipped for this climate.

To enter the temple at Angkor Wat, we must cross a large stone bridge. The width of the bridge is great enough that two cars could easily pass side by side—that's if cars drove here, but it's only foot traffic. On each side of the bridge lay columns of black rock. Many tourists flock to Angkor Wat. The central temple is spectacular. As we cross the moat via the stone bridge, the temple rises in front of us. The spires have the classic Cambodian lotus design.

Lotus.

The symbols repeat and create one more spoke of this wheel of seeming circumstances.

All along the surfaces of the temple, in the walkways and rooms, are images carved into the walls. Images of figures, humans and gods. We're searching for Garuda; only, which is Garuda?

The first day, we wander among the buildings. There are

many people here of many different nationalities.

The group of structures is extensive. Some of the buildings have been restored and some of them are covered in evidence of the voracity of the jungle. Tree roots that grow up and through buildings look to have been poured from above and then hardened. They flow like pale fingers about the stone. Though the image is eerie, it is beautiful in a haunting way.

My focus is on our goal, but this area is so unique. My thoughts continually drift with the seduction of the uncommon beauty.

We end our first full day with nothing to show for it and many buildings still to search. The complex is so vast, even if we knew where to look, we might search for days without finding anything.

At the beginning of our second day in Angkor Wat, I ask Adrien, "What do you think about taking a tour?" He stares at me with slightly glassy eyes. This entire experience is taking a toll on him. He hardly appears to be listening, and even this early in the day, he drags his feet. We'll need to be better prepared and have some additional water to stave off dehydration in this heat. "We'll never be able to locate what we need by ourselves. It's searching a city with no map."

With a nod, Adrien scans the area.

"There, Ellen." He points with a heavy hand toward what appears to be an information center of some sort. "Let us inquire as to when the next tour is."

After speaking with the man at the counter, we're soon standing with a mixed group of people who are milling about waiting for the tour to begin. Their conversations are a hum that accompany the songs of the insects. Our guide arrives, a young Cambodian woman who seems to be in her mid-twenties. She's pretty — beautiful, really — with long, straight black hair and large, luminous brown eyes. She tells us her name is Crystal, and she's worked at Angkor Wat for seven years. Although she's young and soft-spoken, she becomes a general when herding the group together and keeping us on a timetable.

We shuffle through the main complex as Crystal explains where we are.

"Angkor Wat is one of the largest religious monuments ever built. The temple was constructed in the early twelfth century by the Khmer King Suryavarman II as his state temple and capital city. In the beginning, it was dedicated to the Hindi god Vishnu but later, in the twelfth century, became a Buddhist temple as the religion of the people changed." As she speaks, she points to different aspects of the temple we're in. "Many of the surfaces in the temple are covered by images of *devas*, or gods, and *asuras*, or demons. You will see these and many other carvings on our travels through Angkor Wat." Crystal explains that Suryavarman II was a usurper king who came into power by killing his uncle Dharanindravarman I, the former king. As we walk along, she points out an inscription and reads it to us. "It states Suryavarman killed his uncle like Garuda on a mountain ledge would kill a serpent…"

Half listening to her spiel and half wandering farther down the hallway, my ears prick when her words penetrate my consciousness. Garuda? Jackpot!

"Um, Crystal…could you tell us more about Garuda?"

She stops with her mouth half open, and I realize I've

interrupted her prepared narration. She quickly recovers and smiles.

"*Jah*, ma'am. Garuda is a Hindi god. He is the preferred transport of Lord Vishnu. As a winged entity — half man and half bird — Vishnu would ride upon him."

A winged transport?

"I'd be interested in learning more about Garuda. Might you have a moment after the tour to speak with us?"

"*Jah*, ma'am."

For the remainder of the tour, every sound causes me to jump out of my skin, and I gnaw my fingernails down to nothing due to nervousness. I can hardly contain myself and must walk away from the group multiple times to stop from interrupting and demanding Crystal tell me more *right now*. Just as the tour is winding down, an elderly couple from Virginia engage Crystal in a debate about religion.

Patience, Ellen. Patience.

Finally the tour comes to an end and everyone slowly dissipates. Crystal turns toward us.

"Ma'am. You wished to know more about the god Garuda?"

"Yes. To know more of him and to see him. Are there images of him in the temples?"

She nods as she answers. "Oh yes, ma'am. There are many images of Garuda."

Excitement moves through me like a flood, and I reach out to grasp Adrien's arm. We're close. I know we're close.

"Please, Crystal. Could you show us the images?"

She's still nodding at us and gestures for us to follow her back among the temple walls. Many times, she stops to point out a carving or image of a large figure with the head, feet, and wings of a bird of prey, but the torso and arms of a man. Each time I step to the image, lay my hands upon it and wait. Concentration in every motion, I give myself to the image — but again and again nothing happens.

What's wrong? What am I not doing?

As I step back from yet another image with a deep, disappointed sigh, Crystal inches forward.

"Mayhap you would like to see Preah Khan, ma'am?"

"Preah Khan?" With a raise of my eyebrows, I turn to glance at Adrien. He's as lost as me and with a shrug we both look at Crystal. "What is Preah Khan?"

"It's the temple complex next to Angkor Wat. There are many, many images of Garuda at Preah Khan, more than anywhere else."

"Yes." My pulse quickens with the thought of a temple special to Garuda. "Yes, please. Let's go there."

Crystal leads us back to the tour guide building and soon we we're seated in a tuk tuk. A tuk tuk is basically a rickshaw that will seat up to five people, though not comfortably. It's pulled by a small motorcycle. When Crystal, Adrien, and I each climb aboard, the entire thing sways and I think it may tip. It doesn't, however, and soon we're off — at the speed of light. The "road," as Crystal loosely refers to it, is nothing but a dirt path winding through towering trees. There aren't any seat belts in the tuk tuk, and I've got my fingers clenched onto the side rail for dear life. I'm excited to get to Preah Khan, but I'd like to arrive alive.

The jungle is so beautiful and foreign from anything I've known. It captures my attention, and I forget to worry about the ride. The sun filters through the leaves in jagged streaks, which are blinding one moment, gone the next. Though the jungle between Angkor Wat and Preah Khan is not overly dense, there's a thriving population of birds and insects and the air is alive with the calls and buzzing of each. Multiple times, I see a midsized green bird with a grey head. It has a heavy beak and makes a trilling call. The ground cover is sparse, and the trunks of the trees are bare many feet up until the branches leaf out in vibrant green. One good thing about traveling at this speed is that it creates a nice breeze and the day doesn't feel as warm.

During the ride to Preah Khan, Crystal tells us of Garuda's birth from an egg and the story of he and Lord Vishnu meeting.

"Garuda stole the elixir of immortality from the gods' residence. He required it to free his mother from the serpents, who had taken her captive. Along the way, he met Vishnu and was promised immortality, without the elixir, in exchange for becoming Vishnu's mount. At Preah Khan, there are seventy-two statues of Garuda that encircle the outer wall of the temple, and many more within the walls."

The main entrance to Preah Khan is on the eastern side, but we're coming from the opposite direction, so our tuk tuk swings around at the western entrance. Our driver comes to an abrupt halt, which throws the three of us forward in our seat. If I fall to my knees and kiss the ground, I wonder if anyone will notice. As it is, when I step off the cart, my knees shake. I'm happy to be out of the vehicle.

The western gate of Preah Khan is impressive. Awestruck, I stand and stare, wondering what the main entrance must look like. The walkway passes through an arch of a building with three towers in the traditional lotus style.

The path leading up to the arch is lined with stone figures who all have their arms wrapped around a horizontal column. It may be a representation of a snake, but it is so worn I can't tell. The figures are darkened with age, almost black, and most of them are missing their heads. A sense of time pulses off them. Passing through the gateway before us are three Buddhist monks with their orange robes and shaved heads. The stark contrast created by the bright color of their robes and the earth tones of the rock walls is startling.

As we pass through the cutaway into the main complex of the temple, I look up and around. The stone is ancient. Lichen grows on every surface, and the intricate patterns and colors add to the beauty of the area.

Crystal continues to talk as we go. She tells us some more of the history of this temple complex.

"Preah Khan, which means 'Sacred Sword or Holy Sword,' was built in the twelfth century. The temple was quite wealthy with jewels, gold, pearls, and perfumes, among other things. There were more than a hundred thousand people living within its walls, including teachers, dancers, attendants, and servants."

The walk through Preah Khan is fascinating. Much of the temple has been restored, but there are whole sections where the vegetation still rules. Great trees grow out of the stones. The trees don't appear to have any bark and are pale in color. As in Angkor Wat, the trunk and roots look as if they were poured from above and hardened, as opposed to growing from beneath. They resemble large, pale worms surrounding the buildings. A little creepy, yet somehow amazing.

Monuments, statues, reliefs, and etchings are everywhere. Stopping often, I take a closer look at each of them, running my hands over the worn stone. The rock is warmed from the sun, but rough to the touch. I feel relaxed here. No longer so driven to find the Garuda I need and to find it right now. It's as if we're alone in the world. This place is beyond age. I haven't seen the monks since we entered the temple, and the only sounds other than an occasional comment from Crystal are still the calls of birds and hum of insects. It's a step back in time.

Adrien hasn't spoken since we entered Preah Khan. When I look at him, he seems to be doing well. He's sipping his water and studying an image of some *apsaras,* or dancers. These images are abundant on the buildings. There's even a Hall of Dancers.

With slow, even steps, I move down the wall. My hand drags over images of Garuda that line the enclosure. My mind drifts and I'm not thinking of anything, just enjoying the day and the drone of insects mixed with Crystal's stories.

Like a nuclear blast, the flash hits. Suddenly, I'm in a crouched position with no memory of how I got there. The temple walls are gone. With my fingers digging into the soil, my head wrenches back. Arching in a contraction of intense pain, I emit a scream. Flames lick over my skin, causing it to bubble and burst, charring with the heat. Each breath creates an inferno in my lungs. Another shriek, and I'm sure to pass out. I'm finished — the game is over.

Abruptly, mercifully, the light and heat dim slightly. They're still intense but not so excruciating. My body slowly numbs, and the pain becomes bearable.

Breathing. Harsh breaths are the only sounds I hear. Slowly, terrified of what I'll see, I crack open my eyes, surprised I still have the use of them, to peer at my arms. The skin is intact, unchanged. What happened? Immobile with terror, I'm shut down. My brain wants to move, to flee this area and the history of pain, but my body is trapped in fear. Past the point of fight or flight, I'm frozen. The deep beat of my heart pulses in the vein at my wrist, and my eyesight is nothing but a pinpoint.

Move, Ellen.

A deep breath in and out through my nose, and then another, and my heartrate begins to slow. With a fuzzy intensity, my eyesight reaches to the edges of my vision. With an immense effort, I'm able to release my hold on the ground. Carefully, I stretch my fingers and hands as they cramp from their tight position. Another breath, and my back relaxes enough to give an audible crack. On a stiff neck, I slowly pivot my head to glance behind me — first one way and then the other. I'm alone. Where are Adrien and Crystal? Stretching out dark behind me is my shadow, and it's only then I realize the light emanates from something in front of me. I can't make my head turn to look. Fear holds me in its persistent grip. If it keeps the pain away, I'm happy to stay in this crouched, cowed position forever.

Time passes. Nothing changes. I don't move, the light doesn't change. Everything is still; even my breathing is almost silent. I can't truly relax, though, waiting for something. I'm tuned to the lack of bird calls or sounds of insects, something that easily became oppressive so recently. Oh, how I wish for the sound of a bird.

Time passes. I can't stay here forever. My legs and feet are asleep and beginning to cramp. I'm going to have to move, to risk it.

With a small shift to my crouch, I turn toward the light.

Now that I've decided, my adrenaline is again pumping and my fight or flight is ready to go. Slowly, fearfully, I lift my head and move my view from the ground directly in front of me to the area of light.

It's so bright the entire world is nothing but a blur. With a hand to shade my eyes, I peer at what's emitting this brilliantness. Subtly, the light wanes, and I make out the outline of a being.

No way…

My brain must have been fried in the light. How can it be?

In front of me, reaching many feet into the sky, is Garuda. It must be, although I can't quite get the possibility through my head. My eyesight passes over the feet and legs of a bird, up the torso and arms of a man, to its head. The head of a bird of prey. Large, intense black eyes peer down at me, looking over a curved beak designed to tear flesh. His wings of bright yellow are arched behind. He must stand four stories tall. My neck hurts from the angle necessary to see all of him. I stare at him and he stares at me. What am I to do now?

With my body leaning to the side prepared to flee, I stand. Nothing. He continues to regard me with those intense hawk eyes.

A few additional breaths and my adrenaline is dropping; my heartbeat steadying. Courage, like a drug, begins to flow through my veins.

The words of the clue echo in my brain: *advance forward, ever changing, ever growing. Fortitude is cast, despair forsaken.*

Courage. Bravery. Of course.

Head held high, my footsteps bring me closer to Garuda. He shines so bright, the closer I get my eyes begin to water, tears running down my face. When I'm right next to him, I don't stop to think. With a purposeful reach, I grab a handful of feathers and begin to climb. The feathers are slick, and once or twice, falling is a real possibility.

Higher and higher I climb while Garuda stands still as a statue. When I come to his torso, which is covered in skin, I'm not sure what to do, but a whisper on my shoulder causes me to look. His wing is within reach. Planting my feet, with a slight push and twist, I grasp frantically for a hand-hold on his wing and continue up. At the top of his wing, I'm barely astraddle his neck before, with one pump of those powerful wings, we're airborne.

Straight up like an arrow we soar. Crouched down, my arms and legs grasp his neck. My fingers dig into his wings where they join his shoulders. Once again, terror fills me. I like to fly, but come on—not on the back of a large bird-man. For an unknown amount of time I hunch, stuck to his neck like a tick. My breathing puffs out of my chest, and I'm flushed all over, afraid to lift my head. Finally, after a few moments, we level out and it's easier to sit astride his shoulders.

Bravery. With concentration, I repeat the word and instill it into my spirit.

Gingerly, I lift my head from where it's buried among his feathers and gaze around. Nothing but the blue of the sky and below us, billowing clouds. How high are we? Where is he taking me?

The rhythm in the pump of his wings is soothing. Hypnotic. Before too long, I sit up straight, although my thighs still grip tight, and I have a crushing grasp on the feathers at his nape.

The longer we fly, the more relaxed I become until my

fingers fall away from his feathers, sliding out of them like from water. My hands and arms lie against my thighs and my body is limp, shifting subtly with the motion of his flight. As I relax further into the motion, my head falls backward, my eyes blink closed, and my arms outstretch. I am free. There is nothing but the pulse of his wings. Nothing but the wind whistling around us. The sun is warm and bright, the air smells of heaven.

How much time passes? I have no comprehension beyond the now...

With a blink, my consciousness awakens and I become aware of the present, aware of my need to learn something, to receive something. Seemingly, as soon as my perception changes, so does his flight. Sharply, enough to cause me to be thrown forward into his neck again, thrown forward to frantically grasp at him with all my limbs, we begin a steep plummet downward. Everything whites out as we pass through clouds. Moisture from the mist beads my skin. The speed of his flight forces the water to flow backward, driving it into my hair and to fly in splashes off my arms.

Through the clouds, I am able to distinguish the ground — an island.

As if from the shutter of a camera, my view changes. There's a click and we're impossibly closer to the land. No longer am I able to tell I'm over an island; all I see is green. Then another click, and we're over a city. A large city with buildings of varying ages and architecture. Garuda dips one wing and we circle over the top of a steeple. I know this pinnacle. As we circle, a, deep chime rings out.

Big Ben. London.

Then up, higher and higher. Farther into space than we were before. With an ear-deafening screech, he gives a mighty shrug and dislodges me from his shoulders.

A scream of surprise and horror rips from my lungs as gravity latches on and I plummet toward the earth. Terrified, I can't control my fall, and my body spins around and around. My hair obscures everything and my clothes snap as they're caught in the wind. The land rushes up to meet me at an alarming rate, and I shriek again just before impact.

*****

"Ellen?"

The memory of Adrien saying my name is ingrained within me. He's destined to be the one picking up the pieces when my mind shatters with these visitations.

"Ellen."

A deep breath fills my lungs, and my eyes crack open. How long have I been in this prone position? My vision is filled with an immensity of green and yellow grasses, my head buried within them so the closest are without form or definition, out of focus with their nearness. The farthest ones appear sharp to the touch. A brave beetle climbs one stalk, foot over foot, without seeming to have a care in the world. He must be very brave, for with his diminutive size, the grass blade is very tall. My eyes track his movements while the rest of me refuses to move. Just my eyes, my breath, and the beat of my steady heart. When the beetle reaches the end of the stalk of grass, just before it buckles under his weight, he spreads his hidden wings and takes flight. My eyes track him until he's out of sight.

"Ellen?" As always, Adrien's voice is a mixture of worry and calm. How does he pull that off?

"Can you sit up, my dear?" His hand rubs my arm, but I don't have the energy to respond. A shadow blocks the sun, and then Crystal is squatting in front of me, peering down.

"What happened to her? Is she going to be all right?"

"Yes. Yes, she will be fine. Let us just give her a moment, shall we?"

They grow quiet as we wait. Them for me, and me for myself.

My senses waken, and I become increasingly aware of my surroundings: the call of birds, a beetle buzzing — could it be the same one coming back for another look? — and the warmth of the ground. Its heat and firmness. With the solidness of the ground comes a pain in my arm. Not a bad pain, it's not broken, but a discomfort. An ache. As if I'm lying on a rock. With a deep sigh, I roll onto my back, looking blindly into the sky. I stretch the fingers of my opposite hand, flex, and straighten my arm before I reach tentatively across my body to touch the hurt one. There, encircled on my bicep, is something. Something rough and metallic. With a twist, I grasp it in an attempt to spin it on my arm, but it doesn't want to move.

At my touch, the words enter my mind:

A final step to comprehension,
to entrust, to concede.
Time abiding, the essence of life fulfilled, a course set.
A recognition of all that will be.

Adrien moves closer. My vision returns, and it's him I

see instead of the sky as he leans in to look at the bracelet.

"Well, Ellen. What do you have there?"

Scanning my view his way, he raises his brows at me.

Okay, I think. *Rest time is over.*

Giving a push, I sit up cross-legged and keep my hand on the band. With a tip of my head and a lift of my arm, I study it. My eyes confirm what my fingers told me; it's rough. What I couldn't feel is the rust and corrosion. Decay flakes off the metal with each touch. I think it's safe to say this arm band is my token from Garuda. Now to figure out what it means and how to use it with my vision.

My vision. London and Big Ben. Once again, I know where we need to go, but not what we need to do when we get there.

When I push to my feet, an involuntary groan forces its way past my lips. An arch of my back has it cracking and straining. It feels as if many days have passed since we first approached Preah Khan. Seeming to agree, my stomach gives a mighty growl and constricts in upon itself. I need to move, to loosen my muscles and stretch them out. Adrien hands me a bottle of water and with a word of thanks, I take a large gulp. The water is warm, but could there be anything more delicious?

The area we're in is large, about a half-acre. There aren't any other tourists about. This is lucky, as we would probably have drawn attention with me passed out on the ground. Upright, I begin to pace. Adrien's and Crystal's eyes track my every movement.

As my path takes me first by Adrien and Crystal and then away, I reach up and with some effort, slide the armband from my skin. In doing so, I leave a large scrape that wells a deep rivulet of blood.

"Ouch, damn it!" On instinct, I rub the wound with my opposite hand, which only manages to smear blood on my arm, hand, and the bracelet. I feel the change of the metal before my eyes notice. The corrosion and rust are wiping off — wiping off with my blood.

"Okay. That's just freaky." With a swift stride, I approach Adrien to show him what's happening with the metal.

He stands as I near him, and Crystal moves toward us. I have the bracelet in my hands, it and them now covered in my blood. Moving my fingers over its surface, shiny silver is visible where the red smears. With a thrust, I push my hands out to Adrien and Crystal.

"Look at this. Would you just look at this! You both saw what the armband looked like, right? How can it be coming clean? And with blood?"

"Not just blood, Ellen. Your blood." Adrien glances from my eyes back to what's occurring in my hands. "Your blood is wiping the corrosion away."

My body flushes with heat at his words and I open my mouth to say something, but close it without uttering a word. What can I say? Everything since Adrien showed up on my doorstep has been weird, but this is the oddest thing I've experienced yet.

"Here." Crystal steps to us and in her hand is a bottle of water. She hands the water to Adrien and quickly unties a handkerchief from around her neck. We all pause a moment to look at each other, and then rush to wash the blood from the armband. Diluted red runs into the grass and the bracelet sparkles in the sunlight. It's beautiful, intricately braided with silver strands of metallic rope.

My legs shake badly. Fear? Excitement? "I need to sit down." I glance around and, seeing a tree trunk not far away, move unsteadily toward it. Adrien and Crystal follow into the shade of the tree and the three of us sit without speaking. I wait a moment to calm, and then look down at the bracelet in my hand.

"Can one of you explain to me what's going on?" Crystal looks more and more confused as the moments pass.

"Um..." I look at Adrien for guidance. How much should or shouldn't we tell her?

"Of course, Crystal, my dear. But first, let's give Ellen a moment to figure it out herself, shall we?"

She looks as if she doesn't want to do that but refrains from speaking again. She turns toward me and looks pointedly at the bracelet.

With a slightly quaking hand, I hold the bracelet up and give it a good look. It is quite lovely, something I'd gravitate toward in a store. The roping is intricate and realistic, with a smooth inside. As I study the bracelet, my finger runs across something rough on the interior of the piece. The shade of the tree is limiting my exploration. Feeling stronger now, I push up and move back into the bright sunlight. It looks like some kind of writing, but it's not a language I know.

"Crystal? Could you come here and look at something for me?"

As soon as I say her name, she's up and heading my way, eager to have some information. When she's beside me and peering over my shoulder, I turn fully toward her, seeing Adrien is heading to us. I wait until he joins us and then hand the bracelet to her. I have a split second of doubt, possessiveness over the jewelry filling my heart, but then I release it into her grip.

"There's writing of some sort on the interior of the bracelet. Are you able to tell us what it says?"

She doesn't do anything for a moment, just looks me in the eye as if trying to figure out what exactly is going on. Her expression doesn't change, but she looks from me to the piece, turning it this way and that to catch the light.

"I don't understand."

"What? What does it say? What don't you understand?" Now it's me looking over her shoulder at the bracelet as if I'll be able to understand just by looking at it again.

"It's Khmer. It says, 'A World Beyond.'" She looks first at me and then at Adrien and then back to me with a shake of her head. "A World Beyond. But I don't know what that means."

I reach out for the armband, and with some hesitancy, she sets it in my hand. "A World Beyond." With a final glance at the band, I push it back onto my upper arm. I have an idea. A driving, bold idea. One that has been pushing into my mind for some time now. One that I've attempted to ignore, for when I fixate on it, I'm filled with a sense of fear. Fear and awe. Maybe I'm wrong. Maybe they're all wrong. Maybe it won't be required.

"Thank you for your help, Crystal. Adrien, we need to be leaving now. We're heading to London."

"London?"

At the tone of his voice, I stop walking away and turn toward him.

"London, England?"

"Yes, Adrien. London, England."

"But we just came from London. We seem to be going in circles..."

At his words, I give a harsh bark of laughter, which causes his look to intensify. Does he think I'm losing my mind? How little he knows how true his words are and possibly how close his worries are. I know he wants more information, but for now, I shake my head at him and turn away to head out of the park, sure he'll follow. Should I tell him all I know, or think I know? Would it make it easier for him if he's prepared for the final step, or will it just cause him to lose focus? And how will I tell him when the time comes? Will he be able to let go and allow me to do what I'm afraid I must? And if I'm correct, how will I find the courage?

With an inner shake of my head I lengthen my stride. I need to concentrate on getting to the next stop — to the Guardian. If I think too hard on what's ahead of me, I'll falter. I'll fail. And I know now, I mustn't fail.

Chapter 12

D amn it! I want to scream and pull my hair out. We've been in London for two days, and we're still no closer to finding anything of interest. And really, in a city of this size, we could look for a lifetime and never find what we're searching for.

I have no idea what I'm looking for in London. Where do I go? This game is pushing me to the limits. Big Ben was my image from Garuda. Does that simply reference London, or will it have something to do with the clock? Or perhaps

Westminster Abbey itself?

Adrien stayed at our hotel this morning. I needed some time to myself. A simple walk. The parks, or Royal Parks as they're called in London, are breathtaking. The preservation of the land in the heart of this city is incredible, and for me, welcome. Today, as I stroll through St. James Park, my soul is soothed by simply watching the birds on the lake. If I come back tomorrow, I'll need to remember to bring bread to feed the ducks and geese. If I weren't so caught in my own situation, I would laugh at the haughty attitude of the geese while the ducks quibble alongside them. The breeze blows over with a cool intensity, causing my hair to tickle my cheeks. I push the strands out of my eyes and tuck them behind my ear.

Abruptly pulled from my musings, my eyes dart up and across the water to a man standing by a tree. Is he watching me? Why didn't I notice him before? It's not like me to be so absentminded. He's dressed like the men in China—Stephen's men. The black suit is common enough. There are many businessmen and women passing through the park. It's a week day and the rest of the world is working, but still. There's something different about him. His demeanor, or perhaps an intensity he projects. Less like a businessman and more like a soldier.

Moving away from the water and into a line of trees, I work to keep him in sight. As I continue steadily away from him, I scan the area but don't spot anyone else or anything out of place. So much for my peace of mind. All my newfound tranquility is shot in an instant.

St. James Park is heavy with trees, but as I near the Thames River, I'm able to catch glimpses of Big Ben as it towers high above the tree line in the distance. I've been to the tower every day since we arrived, looking for inspiration. I've even taken to carrying the box with the tokens in my bag, and I wear the armband day and night. Though the verses appeared when I first gripped each token, now having them near is the only thing that controls the words from pounding in my brain. The tokens seem to help harness the words. As it is, even with the muting, the lines from the visitations pass through my mind in a constant revolution. I find I can't sleep, can't eat. I must find the Guardian and finish this.

My mind spins with the knowledge I possess, but closes off before the answer to the next verse presents itself. Fear pushes out all thoughts. Is it self-preservation that stops me from seeing the answer? What do I need to do to prepare my mind for the next solution? As if I can outrun my limitations, my footsteps increase their speed until I'm practically breaking into a trot. With my head down, vision on the path in front of me, I don't notice the man until I run headlong into him. Our abrupt impact would have had me sitting on my backside if he hadn't grabbed me by my forearms, steadying me. I look up with a startled gasp into the face of Eric, Stephen's man from the tunnels in Africa.

Uttering a wretched cry, I pull my arms from his grip. Wearing a shocked expression and with a careful step back, I prepare to turn and run. His face, always stoic, is a mask. He gives nothing away as he stands still, taciturn, watching me.

As I spin to flee, I'm faced by three men who've come up silently behind me: Stephen and two more of his followers.

"Ellen. So wonderful to see you again." A large smile splits his pinched face. This is his attempt at being friendly, I'm sure, but somehow all he pulls off is creepy.

My mind races so fast; thoughts fly in and out of my head and I can't grasp them. My pulse jumps to a frantic pace, my heart leaping out of my chest, and beads of sweat dot my upper lip. With an unsteady hand, I wipe over my face, take a deep breath, and push myself to think.

"Stephen." Okay, I'm in a public place. There are people all around — families picnicking, workers on lunch; in the distance, I see two Bobbies strolling along monitoring the activities. I'm barely aware of Stephen as I scan the area looking for a way out. This is a mistake. When he speaks again, it causes me to jump, as I see he's moved closer.

"I knew we'd be together again." He raises his eyebrows at me. With a soft "tsk, tsk" and a wagging of his finger, he admonishes me. "You were a very bad girl, Ellen... Come, we need to talk." He says this and, taking for granted I'll be compliant, reaches for my arm and turns to head away.

Before he can touch me, I step back. "Are you insane? I'm not going anywhere with you." I back myself up a few paces and once again scan the area. "Go away, Stephen. I have nothing to say to you." The heat from Eric's body registers on my back as he steps forward, hemming me in and causing my already racing pulse to escalate. With a quick move, I give a glance over my shoulder at him and turn back to the true threat.

Stephen has the audacity to look offended by my words, but I don't care. Skirting them, I give a sideways look at Eric, turn, and walk quickly away. Twice I glance back, but they don't move. All four watch me go, but I know they'll be back.

Great. I need this on top of everything else.

Now I don't know what to do. Adrien and I can't pack up and run. I need to be here. I must solve the clue. My calm is shattered. I may as well continue with my plans and head toward the river. I'd decided to go to the river side of Westminster and see if I notice anything different about the tower. I would like to get inside and to the top, but that's a no-go for a non-national.

On the north side of Westminster Abbey, with the tower in front of me and the Thames on one side, I crane my neck back to look up at the clock face. It's nearing noon, and when the hour hits, the bell will ring. Between scanning the tower for anything interesting and watching for Stephen and his men, I misstep and accidently trip off a curb, almost twisting my ankle in the process.

"Damn it." As I bend down to rub my ankle and berate myself about being clumsy, my attention is caught by the motion of a cruise boat on the river. Almost immediately, a flash at the building on the other bank catches my eye and has me standing slowly. The building undulates as if bulging from the screen of life. The quiet is so intense, it's like a vacuum has occurred, and the pressure and tingling in my head is almost painful. With a quick blink, I rub my eyes and peer again. Everything is back to normal. Behind me are the calls of children at play and the honking of horns.

What is that building?

A smartly dressed man strolls past me, heading down the street. With a jump, I stop him. "Excuse me, sir."

He looks at me as if I might be dangerous, so I put on my best innocent face and give him a big grin.

…but not too big, Ellen. You don't want him thinking you're a maniac. With a stiff arm, I point across the river. "Can you tell me what that building is? The large one across the Thames?"

He looks in the direction I'm pointing and turns back to me.

"County Hall, miss. That building is County Hall."

"County Hall." I nod my head to indicate my understanding and as he turns to continue to his destination, I yell out a belated, "Thank you."

I need to get across the river to County Hall. With a quick glance around, I remember Westminster Bridge is right on the other side of my location. Westminster Abbey and Big Ben sit on the edge of the river. From here, foot traffic as well as vehicles cross the bridge. It appears to be about a fifteen-minute walk between the two buildings. Maybe I should go back to the hotel and get Adrien. But no, I decide, I'll continue on my own. If I find something, we can always come back.

The wind picks up as I cross the Thames. It smells faintly of water and fish, but isn't completely unpleasant.

My attention is divided between not running into other people crossing the bridge and keeping an eye around me to watch for men in black suits. When looking back, the image of Westminster Abbey and the tower of Big Ben catch my attention. How beautiful and majestic. In my mind's eye, I again see the image of them from the back of Garuda as we circled high above. This is definitely the time and place, just...what am I supposed to find? And when I find it, I'm all too afraid I know what I'm supposed to do. Will I be able to fulfill my part in the prophecy?

With a forceful shove, I mentally push my apprehension out of my thoughts and continue across the bridge. *Just keep moving, Ellen.* Cars drive past, bringing with them the occasional whiff of exhaust and a blare of horns in the distance. The sidewalks on either side of the road are heavy with foot traffic. London is a great city to walk in.

Halfway across, my focus intensifies on the building I'm moving toward. Closer and closer I get. County Hall. Why this building? Why didn't Garuda show me this building if it's to play a part in this venture?

County Hall is a big building and fills a couple blocks. There's a main thoroughfare, running along the land side of it, filled with traffic. Beyond County Hall, the Eye raises above the Thames. The large Ferris wheel might make for a spectacular view of London and this area I'm hunting. I put this information in the back of my mind for further contemplation. Maybe a ride on the Eye will be illuminating...

Westminster Bridge ends, and I turn east along Belvedere Road. This lane fronts County Hall, so I'll keep my eyes open for anything—anything at all that calls to me or looks even slightly out of place. So far, there is nothing. County Hall has many interesting sculptures at set intervals throughout the exterior. I've never seen so many statues as walking through London. The city's parks and buildings are covered in them. The art exhibited on this building is unique. There are sculptures of humans but still different—interesting, in odd poses or bearings. At the corner of the building, a left turn has me heading for the Eye. My attention is drawn to it. A staggering amount of activity surrounds it with people, and wares being bought and sold. It's one of the largest Ferris wheels in the world, and being this close to it is shocking to my already traumatized senses.

With a mental shake, the path is again in my sights and making a turn at the next corner of the County Hall, I'm heading down the River Thames on the Queen's Walk. Behind me on the pathway are large, mature trees and benches to sit and take in the sights of the river. The way I'm heading continues with a pathway past the large front of the building. It's twice as wide as the rest of the lane and spacious. Many people stroll here and visit the stores for shopping and eating. The building, on the river side, is cut out in the shape of an amphitheater. In my mind, I see the Sanctuary of Fortuna in Italy. The two buildings are built alike. I'm constantly surrounded by themes that circle over and over. Around me, the hum of conversation reminds me of the droning of bees and is strangely soothing.

When I reach the end of the walking path, I'm back at this side of Westminster Bridge and there's nowhere left to go. I've made a complete circuit around County Hall to no avail.

This excursion to give me time to think hasn't worked. I'm more confused than before. Adrien is sure to be worried by now. I'd best head back.

St James's park is even quieter on my return trip. There aren't any men in black suits to disrupt the peace, and in no time at all our hotel is reached. Where might Stephen and his men have gone? When will they pop up to cause more disruption?

*****

As expected, Adrien is pacing by the time I enter our room. With the door closed behind me, I wait for his explosion, but he's eerily calm.

"Where have you been all this time?"

"I was out walking. I told you, I needed some fresh air and some time to think." I need him on guard, so in the interest of full disclosure, I tell him about my new encounter with Stephen and his men.

He approaches me, shaking his head, a disappointed look on his face. "Ellen. The pressure on you is great, I know, but you can't disappear. We knew Stephen would show up again at some point. I told you, he's crafty and persistent. What if he had taken you? Where would I even begin to search?"

"I know, Adrien. I know. I'm just trying to work through some things."

"Let me help you. Talk to me. You're keeping everything inside and it is eating you up."

Nodding my head, the pressure bubble I've been living with bursts, and tears fill my eyes. My voice comes out in a whisper. "I'm scared, Adrien."

His expression softens as he steps forward, taking me into his arms. At the warm, fatherly touch, I burrow into him, holding on tight. My breath catches in a sob, and he pats my shoulder, uttering small soothing sounds. After a moment, he pulls back and with my hand in his, leads me to the sitting area.

"Sit," he instructs. The couch is soft, and he brings me a cool glass of water.

"Now. Talk to me. Tell me what ideas are swirling around in your brain that have you so afraid."

With a deep breath, I walk Adrien through the concepts that are coming together and the significance of what they mean.

"When we first discussed the prophecy, I thought it was interesting and kind of disconcerting I didn't remember it until you began to speak it. My brain felt like someone else had tapped into it when the flood of words came rushing in.

Suddenly, I remembered — and not only that — I recalled learning it. Sitting with my mother and father, but not just them. A whole host of people and other children. Who were those children, Adrien?"

"All our children are taught the words of the prophecy. Not all will have promise of being part of it. In fact, most won't. We've been searching for the Key for long before my time. Everyone learns so the words can be passed on to the next generation, and the next."

"Why didn't I remember it until you said it?"

"I don't know. Maybe, when you forced your abilities to stop developing, you forced the memories out, too."

Nodding but not sure if I agree, I mutter, "Maybe." With a shift toward him, my thoughts and words continue. "The mission of the prophecy is to fill a new position in a gathering of individuals, entities. A circling of bodies, philosophies, lives."

He inclines his head in agreement. "That is so. From time past, our assemblage has agreed these entities are spirits; gods, perhaps."

"Do you really think that, Adrien? A gathering of gods?"

"Conceivably."

"Okay. So, the prophecy talks about a gathering of gods. Circling. Always circling. But watching, unable to change anything."

"Yes."

"You know, so many things in life are a circle. It's the fundamental motion of the world. The galaxy. The universe. Back to an atom and smaller."

He nods as my ideas flow, not interrupting.

"All the way out from the universe, and back to the

wheel—the swastika, where we started."

"Yes, Ellen. Turning, always turning."

"Then we have the words from the spirits. Not just verses. not just random, but clues. Clues that will lead us to the Guardian."

Touching one index finger with the other, he says, "Faith was the first."

"Faith and then imagination and then choice."

"Choice?" His eyebrows pull together and his stare holds my gaze.

With a small motion of my head I answer, "The solution to the riddle of the tarot was choice. It was the answer when faced with the oracle at the Temple of Fortuna. But Adrien, it was more than choosing to select some tiles. Choosing to move on to another challenge, another spirit."

"What was it?"

"Do you remember, when I woke, I was crying?"

"Yes. You wouldn't tell me then what made you cry. Will you tell me now?"

"Of course. I only kept it from you then because it was so new. The concept needed time to settle in my mind. Anyway, when I was with the oracle, part of what she wanted was a commitment. For me to make a choice to become the Key. To accept my place in this game and not look back. I did, and it was grief for the loss of the life I had that had me crying."

"Ellen. I'm sorry you are not able to continue in your life as it was." He pats my hand in a gesture that comforts me.

"The grief was for the possibilities that life once held. The decision to release a normal life—to exchange it for something different. Once I decided to embrace my destiny as the Key, there was no going back. And it's more than that.

Truth be told, I haven't been happy in my life; I was simply existing."

Surprise blooms on his face at my words. "I never knew that, my dear. You should have said something."

"What could you have done for me?" With a shake of my head, I push away the bad feelings and the memories. "There's more to the emotions from the oracle. It was more than grief. There was...I don't know...exaltation." This description comes out with a little shrug. "Excitement to be part of something bigger than myself." Now, I smile at him. "In that cave, with that ancient woman, I made my choice and I became the Key."

Adrien's gaze locks onto me as he listens. His attention is absolute. "So it was choice...but what about the final line that took us to Rome? Do you know what it means to glimpse through the veil?"

"Well, I think that has to do with seeing the world of the Guardians, but perhaps it also helped me to figure out the clue from Anansi, the man-spider in Africa—helped us to get to the Temple of Fortuna. On board the ship, I opened myself, saw things in a whole new and different way. It helped me solve the clue and gave me direction where to go."

"I knew something happened aboard the ship. Something that lead us to Rome. You never explained it to me."

I watch him, my thoughts muddled. How much should I tell him about my vision of Jupiter. He'll never doubt anything about our path. For now, though, I'd like to keep that experience to myself. I can still feel it, the opening of my senses. It was incredible. "Can we not get into that right now? Maybe later?"

"Of course." Sitting back into the couch, Adrien gives me his full attention. "So back to what we were discussing..."

"Yes. So the choice was made—I decided to commit and become the Key. And as you know, the tiles led us to Cambodia and Garuda, but the oracle gave me a clue to help me there. I was very glad to have it, too. With Garuda there was pain—such intense pain. A purifying, perhaps." At this thought, a new thought, my vision turns inward. Could there be a purifying happening with each of the visitations? I'll need to put my mind to that later, after I have some food and rest. When my mind isn't so foggy.

"The verse from the oracle...?"

"Advance forward, ever changing, ever growing. Fortitude is cast, despair forsaken."

"And you understood this? This clue?"

"Not at first, of course. But, as I cowered before Garuda, feeling broken, burnt, and bloody, the answer came to me." When I look at him, the directness and intensity of his eyes urges me to continue. "Bravery."

"Bravery," he repeats in a soft voice.

"Yep. Bravery. So, I got up and forced myself to confront a god."

"You certainly gave us a scare that day. I've had you faint on me, but in Cambodia it was more as if you were convulsing."

"Really? You never told me that." What a scary thought that is. It's bad enough to be in a fugue state during these episodes, but the thought of a seizure? Well...I don't even want to think about it.

"Crystal and I were both scared and anxious for your safety. But then you calmed, and after a bit, you came back to us."

I don't really know what to say to this revelation. As is my nature, when I'm nervous, I pace, and when I find myself on my feet, performing laps in the room, I'm not surprised.

Getting us back on track, Adrien says, "So, Garuda..."

"Ah, yes. What an experience that was. I would like to tell you all of it, but I don't know if I'd be able to come up with adequate words to explain the wonder."

"When did you receive a clue from Garuda? Did you wake to know it?"

"No. No, it was when I wrapped my hand around the armband. That's how it's worked with all the tokens from all the spirits. When I hold it, touch it, the vision comes."

"And what were you told?"

"A final step to comprehension, to entrust, to concede. Time abiding, the essence of life fulfilled, a course set. A recognition of all that will be."

"Well," he breathes. "That certainly sounds as if we are coming to the end."

"It does, doesn't it?" A bit disheartened, I flop down on the couch beside him. "Of course, once again, I don't know what it means."

With a pat of my knee and a small chuckle, he states, "As with all the others, I'm sure when the time comes, you'll figure it out. So, your bigger picture, like a jigsaw puzzle, is coming together."

I give him a nod. "One idea playing into another to build on the final theme." Fear snakes through me and whispers down my spine. The final theme is a mystery that, as of yet, I'm unable to articulate my dread of. I don't know if I'll ever be able to.

"Okay. So far we have faith, imagination, and choice. Then bravery. All traits that make us stronger—even in this world."

He blinks at me, and although I know he's trying to understand—to help me figure out every nuance of these clues—he eyes me with a vacant stare. It causes me to break into laughter.

"I know, right? My brain and my body are tired." I wipe my hands over my face.

"We'll figure it out, Ellen. We're together and we'll deal with this together. You are the Key. The Key will lead the way to the Guardian. All of this is your road map to the final destination."

My head moves in a slight nod, but in truth, I doubt either of us will have much input in our place in all of this.

"Okay," Adrien says and jumps from the couch, grabbing my hands and pulling me up after him. "I think we need to get out and get some air. Maybe stop at a café and get a bite to eat."

With a glance around the hotel room, the stuffy air registers and my stomach growls in agreement. "That would be wonderful."

*****

Adrien and I wander down the streets of London, looking at the architecture and the diversity of people. We try to talk about daily nonsense and stay off the subject of the prophecy or the clues. The sun begins to set as we cross Green Park, heading toward Buckingham Palace. In the distance, the palace shines like a jewel. All the lights are on, both on the exterior of the palace and on the Victoria Memorial in front of Buckingham.

"Ah, it appears the queen is not in residence."

In confusion, I stop and crinkle my brows at him. He gives a small chuckle, takes my arm, and continues. "You see, Ellen, when the queen is in the palace, the flag is flown." He points toward the palace. "No flag, no queen."

"Um... Have I ever told you that you know some of the weirdest trivia?"

Our stroll continues as we pass in front of Buckingham Palace and head toward the river. My mood and soul calm just by being with Adrien. Why did I ever think it would be a good idea to shut him out? Our conversation consists of good-natured comments about people we see and making up stories to explain why they would be out on the streets in London.

St. James Park is on our left as we move toward Westminster Abbey. If I thought Buckingham Palace glowed in the fading light, Westminster is a whole 'nother animal. It's ablaze with lights that highlight its length and the tower of Big Ben.

As if he senses my lightening mood and my ability to process our situation, Adrien returns to the previous subject. "So have you discovered anything new since we've been in London?"

Understanding it's time to buckle down and figure this out, I allow the subject to become serious again. "I have an idea. It's very new though and I'm not ready to talk about it yet. I will tell you it has to do with the original prophecy and what that means not only for mankind but possibly for the entire universe. Please understand, I need to process this."

I know Adrien's questions—his interest in finding the

answer—ultimately aid me in my search for answers and I respect his motives as he probes once more. "Something with the entities? The spirits or gods?"

"Possibly. I have to give it some more thought."

We near Westminster Abbey and Adrien stops to scan the building. "You've been coming here every day, haven't you?"

"Today, while I was out by myself, I was given a suggestion, I think. A hint. When I was kneeling by Westminster, I was drawn to that building across the Thames." My arm raises, and I point out County Hall. "I walked there to check it out, but nothing came of it."

"Are you ready to call it a night or would you like to try again? Perhaps something will show itself."

"Perhaps. Sure, let's do it. I'm unable to sleep anyway."

This time, the trip across the bridge is different. Not only are the buildings lit, but the bridge is also, and the lights reflect upon the water like a wonderland. Everything is magical. Adrien and I stroll, arm in arm, and continue to talk about mundane things, easy things. People walk with us and by us, but the rush of the day is gone. Now everyone seems to stroll. The mood is heady with laughter and ease. The cool breeze off the water only enhances the feeling of relaxation.

When we reach the opposite side of the bridge, instead of working our way around the outside of County Hall as I did before, we go the reverse direction walking down the Queen's Walk toward the Eye. The magic of the area intensifies when I see the Eye is illuminated with purple lights, and County Hall has a different display of light brightening each section. All the colors cast reflections on the river and make it look like a rainbow come down to Earth.

Spotting a coffee house, I pull Adrien and good-naturedly implore him until he treats me to a drink. With our cups in hand, we laugh and joke as we pass the Eye and make the turn at the corner of the building.

Everything stops as my body freezes, my vision captured by the image in front of me. My drink hits the ground and splashes over my boots and pant legs, but I don't notice.

"Ellen! Are you all right?"

Adrien straddles the mess of my coffee and grips me by the upper arms, shaking gently. I can't see anything but the sculpture. How did I miss it before? No, I didn't miss it — it couldn't have looked like this.

A glowing orb outside the second-story window mesmerizes me, and it's a moment before I even notice the truly freaky part of it all. Around the orb are three men. Naked men with no faces, but they're looking right at me, staring at me. I'm hypnotized. Adrien is talking, but his voice is a low hum to my ears.

As I watch, one of the men beckons me with a gesture of his hand. The other two move forward, leaning over him, leaning down to reach for me. Somehow, I'm closer. My neck is craned back and I'm reaching for them when Adrien spins me around.

"Ellen!" he yells at me, effectively breaking the spell.

Blinking rapidly, I glance from Adrien to the now static, dark sculpture. *What. The. Hell?*

"Did you see that, Adrien?"

"See what? What just happened?"

"Oh my God! I feel as though I'm losing my mind." Crouching down, right on the walkway, I stare without focus

186

at the ground until Adrien grabs my arm again and forcibly pulls me to my feet. With his arm around my waist, he quickly walks me back to the bridge, across it, and to our hotel. The entire time, I'm like a zombie, allowing him to direct where I go. Had he walked me off the edge of the bridge, I would have let him. We don't speak the entire trip back to our room and even when we arrive, I'm mute. Adrien sits me on my bed, takes off my boots, and puts me under the covers. My head doesn't even hit the pillow before I'm out, unconscious.

*****

The next day, I wake periodically to see Adrien sitting in one of the hotel chairs, watching me. Twice, I accept a sip of water, but for the most part I'm burnt out. I can't concentrate and just want to sleep. When I do have a moment of awareness, the image of those three, gray-cast, faceless men reaching for me invades my mind, causing me to pull back and drift once again into oblivion. The only way I can battle the fear and dread of this visitation is to shut down. For right now, I've hit my limit.

The sun sinks in the west again before I pull myself out of my self-imposed oblivion. Like coming out of a coma, I'm foggy, my eyes dry and scratchy. I swing my legs over the side of the bed and look around. I'm alone. A huge stretch cracks my back and causes a sigh to escape my lips. After I use the bathroom, I pace slowly around the hotel room to loosen my muscles while deciding what to do.

A few minutes more and still no Adrien. I have my boots on, and after leaving him a short note, I head out the door. I must go back to County Hall. I need to see if the sculpture is still there and still as it was. I'm no longer afraid. I guess, through my sleep, I've come to terms with what's going to be required.

It's full dark when I come around the corner of County Hall. A multitude of tourists still mill around, but they don't bother me. I'm focused.

Immediately, my sight is captured by the glow of the orb, and as a set of three heads swivel toward me, I'm consumed by a fire of affinity for these beings. The fear is gone, as if it never was, and in its place is warmth. How they project so much emotion without facial features is beyond me, but I know they've been on a silent vigil—waiting patiently for my return.

Now, as before, one of the granite men beckons to me. He leans heavily on one arm and gestures in a come-hither motion. My footsteps slow as I near, but my commitment doesn't waiver. The nearer I get, the farther down and toward me he leans. When I arrive at the area directly under the sculpture, three faces peer down at me. Three sets of hands reach for me. All I have to do is stretch across the span separating us. With a flex of my toes, I lengthen my body to its utmost height, my arms outstretched, pulling at the shoulders. I want this—I want this so badly.

When the cold of their grips encounters my overheated skin, a shiver runs down my spine. Suddenly I'm airborne, weightless, floating upward as I'm pulled to them with no obvious effort on their part. The three of them stand as I'm drawn up to face them. Gently, they set me upon the platform of their sculpture. Though they take a step back, my hands and arms are still within their grasps. They emote a feeling of adoration. I am loved. I am adored. After a moment, I gently remove my hands from their relaxed grips and, like a mother, place my palms to their cheeks, one after another. I love them in return.

The sensation of a tear rolling down my cheek surprises me out of this reverie. Blinking rapidly, I reach up to catch another tear when it spills over to trace a path down my face. With a catch in my breath, I watch as the triad of stone men step back, and once again, my attention is caught by the glowing orb behind them. I'm drawn to it. I want to bask in its brilliance forever.

Step by step, I move toward the ball, and with every pace the men fall backward, dropping to their knees, allowing me free access. When next to it, I lay my palms flat upon the surface. The light and heat immediately grow in intensity until I'm screaming into the night.

Chapter 13

The late afternoon sun streaks through the open window as I gingerly open my eyes. The brightness causes me to squint, and my eyes tear. Is it my imagination, or is the light more intense somehow?

Where am I? It's my first thought as my sight pivots around the area. Right behind this thought is the knowledge I'm in our hotel room—mine and Adrien's. With a push, I sit upright to swing my legs over the side of the bed and look around. A sense of vertigo hits, and my body sways slightly.

My head feels too heavy for my neck and falls to the back before I straighten it and my spine. *Okay. How did I get here?* My entire being is filled with a bizarre mixture of nausea and energy. It's like a full-body buzz. With a glance down at my hands, I'm surprised to see they're not shaking. My inner quiver is so powerful, it should manifest in the physical. Everything is the same, yet somehow different. Clearer. Like high-definition television. So defined, I'm having trouble getting my eyes to focus on each item in the room.

The clunk of a drawer closing in the bathroom catches my attention, and when the door opens, Adrien steps out. I glance at him and then back to my hands. After he exits the doorway, he approaches with hesitancy to kneel in front of me.

"Ellen." Gently he lays a hand on my knee, causing me to look him in the eye. "*Oh mon Dieu!* Ellen..." He leans forward even closer and puts a knuckle under my chin to tilt my head into the light. "Your eyes...beautiful." The last word is whispered with reverence.

A bolt of adrenaline hits my system at his words, intensifying the nausea. Visions of horrors fill my mind. What's happened to my eyes?

"What?" I stand so suddenly, he's knocked backward and lands on his backside. Standing so quickly has brought a new wave of dizziness with it but, when I got up, the nausea went away as if it had never been. For a moment, I sway on my feet, and then, with no regard for Adrien's position on the floor, I step over his legs to head into the bathroom and over to the mirror while he scrambles to his feet to follow.

My forward momentum halts at the doorway of the bathroom. With my hand on the light switch, I stop. What am

I going to see? Beautiful, he said, but still the grind of fear sits in the pit of my stomach. I feel Adrien's heat behind me, his presence pressure and reassurance all in one. Tightening my body and mind in an almost physical fist, I grasp my courage and, clicking on the light, step into the bathroom.

The light is harsh as I lean over the sink and push my face up to the mirror. Even with the washed-out effect of the light on my complexion, I see my normally hazel-green eyes are a steely gray in color. Around the pupil is an even lighter circle of silver. In this light, the silver seems to glow. Freaky. But he's right—they are beautiful. My thoughts flash back to the granite statue of the three men—their cast is repeated in my eyes.

The memory of their stony touches, the overwhelming love, the orb—its heat searing me until I was no more...now I know. Now I know it all. My mind is open and my path is before me, but where to go? How do I finish this? The final riddle I've been given plays out in my mind, familiar and welcoming in the way of a mother's hug.

"Ellen? Ellen, how are you feeling?"

How am I feeling? That's a good question. Without speaking, my thoughts turn inward, taking an assessment. I'm still buzzing, but I feel good—really good. Strong. Powerful. Settled.

"I'm good, Adrien." As I catch his eye in the mirror, his drawn brows and worried grimace shows me he's doubtful of my words. "Really. I'm hungry."

My physical need for nourishment seems to soothe him, a normalcy that gives him something to do.

"I'll order us some room service. Then perhaps we can visit."

"That sounds good. Real good. I think I'm gonna jump in the shower. Center my thoughts. And then we can eat and talk."

He gives me one of his long, assessing looks again, but nods and heads out of the bathroom.

"Hey, Adrien?"

At my words, he turns back toward me.

"How did I get here?"

"Take your shower and we'll talk." He silently closes the door behind him.

I spend a considerable amount of time in the shower. Every experience is new. The sound of the water hitting the tiles, the reflection of the droplets in the light. Before I even get in, I'm spellbound. An uncontrollable gasp escapes my lips as the liquid hits my bare skin. The sensations are unlike anything I've experienced before. It's long moments before I pull my head out of the euphoria and begin to wash. Immediately, I'm yanked back in — the feel of the smooth soap, its smell of crushed flowers. A giggle escapes my lips as I work the shampoo into my short curls. My eyes close in ecstasy. This new reality has me seduced. I'm much more than I was.

Turning into the falling water to rinse, I cup my hands and concentrate on the liquid. The cells separate and welcome me in. A universe. Infinity in the palm of my hand. Such a simple thing, and so complex. With an effort, I pull my mind out of this spiral I could easily take. The temptation of knowledge. To delve into the vastness of creation and leave everything else behind. But in my mind and heart, I know I have a bigger part to play and can't dawdle overlong.

Even as the water begins to cool, I hesitate to leave the

shower. It's the thought of what I'll experience next that has me moving.

Water off and toweled dry, I fixate on the feel of the towel against my skin and the cold tile on the bottom of my feet. At one point, I drop to my hands and knees to place my cheek against the cool floor.

Instead of lessening, the onslaught of sensations intensify. How will I control this? Will I be strong enough to not lose myself in the marvels I've found?

While I was in the shower, Adrien dropped clean clothing just inside the bathroom door. So like him to be looking out for me. Have I ever told him how much he means to me? I love him — more than a father, really. He's become a best friend, a confidant. What will he think of the choices I must make, choices I've become committed to?

Pulling on my clothes takes me longer than normal. My skin is hyper-sensitive and every sensation has me stopping to assess it. Some are almost painful in their intensity.

When I exit the bathroom, evidence of the time I took is there, as the food has arrived and Adrien has a pleasant table set for us. The television in the room is on low, a news channel running through daily information, the drone of the people a welcome background in the room. The scents are intoxicating. Drawn toward the food, I sit and waste no time diving into the pasta dish he ordered for me. My body is ravenous. With my mouth full, I sit back and close my eyes in ecstasy, chewing slowly.

"Ellen."

In a fog of pleasure, my eyes open to slits and I gaze at Adrien.

"What are you experiencing? Can you tell me what is

happening?"

How can I ever explain the unexplainable? My mind can't grasp it all, and I'm the one experiencing it.

Giving myself another moment to think, I swallow my pasta and take a drink of tea — wonderful tea! For a moment, the sparkling of the ice cubes in the amber liquid sidetracks my thoughts.

"Ellen?"

Pulling myself from a contemplation of the ice cubes, I give Adrien a small smile and ponder how best to explain what I'm feeling. "Honestly, I don't know what to tell you. How do I explain something when I'm not sure what's happening? What am I experiencing? Everything, Adrien. Everything." He hangs on every word, and I want so badly to give him something, some tangible information. "I'm seeing, hearing, and feeling everything. My senses are opened, and it's as if I'm a sponge sucking the universe in...or something. I can't tell you why or how this is, just that it is." With a pause, I try to corral my thoughts and give him information. "We have one more stop."

When I say this, Adrien sits up straighter and leans forward.

"You know this? Where is this stop?"

Sucking in a lungful of air, I shake my head at him. "I don't know. I have the final riddle, and I'm certain it's the final one. And I have an image, but it's not something — somewhere — I've ever seen before. As of yet, I don't know what any of it means."

"Tell me the riddle. Perhaps I can make something out of it."

"Okay. Okay." With a push of my feet my chair scoots

back, and with a small clearing of my throat I say:

"Square but not square;
in the closing, a needle shall point the way.
Laid at her foothold, a circle is created and the Key opens a gate.
The new guard plays eternal."

Adrien looks introspective and a bit confused. "Square but not square?"

"I know; I know... What's that supposed to mean?"

We're both deep in thought when I remember my earlier question. "So, Adrien, how did I get here? My last memory before waking in my bed was being at the statue."

Setting down his fork, he reaches for his cup, nodding slightly. "I found you last night. You were sitting on a bench on the Queen's Walk. When I spoke to you, you didn't respond—simply stared out into the Thames."

I push farther back from the table to hear his tale. I don't remember any of this, and he has my full attention.

"I got you to your feet and walked you back here. You went with me easily, but it was as if you were lost within your own mind. I'm thankful Stephen or his men didn't find you in that state. You could have woken up somewhere much different."

"Yeah, great," I wrinkle my nose at the thought. "Thanks, Adrien. That's reassuring."

He gives me a shrug, and we both know he's right. I need to quit taking risks with myself.

With renewed vigor, I return to my meal. My frame is like an empty vessel that doesn't want to be filled. How many calories am I burning in this new, heightened state? As I chew thoughtfully, the hum of the television invades my thoughts. Pushing it away, I continue to eat, gazing out the window at the sun and buildings beyond. But as if it's a persistent fly, the murmur of the machine pushes at me. Feeling slightly irritated, I swing in my chair, planning to turn the TV off, when the story catches my attention. It's not so much the words as the images. With a shift, I stand and walk toward the television, transfixed by the story. Adrien comes up behind me, looking from me to the screen.

Silently, I lift an arm to point at the picture.

"That's it. That's the image in my mind. The circle, marked out like a wheel." Drifting closer to the TV, I grab the remote and push the volume to turn up the sound. Just as I finish, the picture cuts away. The announcers take a moment to discuss the previous story, giving me all the information I need.

"So, once again, the Vatican will be releasing a limited edition of special papal stamps to try to raise money for the fourteen-million-euro restoration of the magnificent colonnades that embrace St. Peter's Square."

The woman next to him nods in agreement. "Yes, Steve. What a great commemoration and a great cause. We'll be right back with Maggie and the weather after a message from our sponsors."

"St. Peter's Square. Vatican City, Italy."

"St. Peter's Square," Adrien repeats.

"A square that isn't a square..." With a raised eyebrow, I gaze at Adrien.

He nods his head in agreement and, walking toward the bed, bends to begin packing his bag. I turn back to the television, seeing the image that was in my mind. Slowly, I nod to myself.

St Peter's Square, here I come.

Chapter 14

We're unable to get a flight out until the next morning, and with my senses open to everything, the last thing I want to do is stay in our room.

"Let's go for a walk. I want to take in the sights — it can only help me learn to control the input of all the stimuli in the world. At times, it's completely overwhelming."

"Of course. A little night air will be good for us both."

When we exit the hotel, night has completely fallen and once again the city sparkles with lights. A cool breeze has picked up and the sounds of the city have intensified in the dark. The honking of cars and hum of traffic echo off the buildings, and in the distance, I swear I can hear the river. At first I think I'm being fanciful, but with my greater sight, taste, and every sensation on my skin, it's only logical my hearing has also been affected.

The streets of London are almost quaint, though I don't know if its citizens would like to hear it described as such. I love this city.

Tonight, we decide to head the opposite direction.

Strolling through Hyde Park is incredible anytime, but at night it's truly magical. The parkways are lit by large, round-topped lanterns, whose light spills onto the cobblestone paths. People are everywhere: walking down the lanes, sitting on the multitude of ready benches, tossing stones into the lake, and even occasionally sneaking out of or into some dark corner. Adrien and I amble along, arm in arm, and I feel truly relaxed for the first time in a long time.

"Ah. I tell you, Adrien, I love this city."

"Yes. London has an enchanting quality."

We walk silently for perhaps an hour. We are just turning back to our hotel when I hear music coming from within a copse of trees along a darkened path.

"Do you hear that?"

"What? What is it?"

"I hear music." With a smile, I turn to him. "Let's find out where it's coming from, shall we?"

"Whatever you would like, my dear. This will be our last night in London—let's do it up right." The last of his sentence was said with a bad southern drawl, which causes me to laugh at him and lean in to give him a brief hug.

We head into the darkened area of the park, following the sound of the music. After walking for a while, I feel confusion and worry creep into my mind. We seem to be walking in circles. I can't locate where the sound is coming from. I move ahead of Adrien when I hear a muffled *humph* from behind me and turn just in time to see a suited man grab Adrien around the throat with his arm. The man lifts him off his feet and begins to pull him into the deeper trees. His attempt at abduction is slowed by Adrien's struggles against him.

Without any thought for my own safety, I run toward the departing men and with the full force of my advancing body, I bring my elbow up to bear—directly into the nose of our assailant. My blow snaps his head back, and as he loses his footing to fall backward, he takes Adrien with him. Forward momentum has me tripping over them both and barely keeping my feet. Swiveling about, I hurry back to lean over the two prone men. I grab Adrien's arm to assist him from the ground. The mystery man has been knocked unconscious; I feel a spark of pleasure at the sight of blood running from his obviously broken nose. When nose meets elbow, elbow wins every time.

"Come on, Adrien. Let's get out of here," I whisper close to his ear. Who knows how many more of Stephen's men are in these woods.

Before we've taken even two steps, a shot rings out, and Adrien falls with a solid *thunk.*   At the sound of the shot, I ducked behind a tree, but now, seeing him down, I drop to my belly and scramble beside him. He's lying on his front and struggling to turn, and with effort I help him onto his back. Scanning the area with my senses, I wait for another attack, but the forest is quiet. Too quiet. Adrien grasps my arm, and with my attention back on him, I'm shocked how pale he already is. It's dark, but even with limited light, I see the blood staining his shirt and puddling under him.

"*Adrien*! Adrien, hold on!" Instinctively, I put pressure on the entry wound, covering my hands in the wetness. It continues to seep from between my fingers, so I push myself to my knees and prepare to stand. "I'll get help. Just hold on."

He shakes his head violently, and with a surprisingly strong grip, he pulls me toward him.

"No." His voice is faint, and I lean over to catch his words. "No, *ma fille*. There is no help for me."

"What? No, Adrien. You'll be fine." Now, it's me shaking my head at him. I try to pull away from him, afraid of what he's saying and not willing to believe it. His lips move, but I can't hear him, and instead of running for help, I'm back on my knees to lean close and hear his words.

"Finish this quest. You are strong—finish what must be done." He reaches up with a shaking hand and for a moment holds onto my medallion, which hangs from my neck, leaving a streak of blood covering it. Off in the distance, I hear the crunch of a branch under a heavy foot. Adrien hears it too, his eyes filling with fear. He pulls me firmly to him and in an insistent whisper, rasps in my ear. "*Run*. Run, Ellen. They're coming."

"No, Adrien. I won't leave you." With a firm grip on his arms, I drag him into a sitting position, causing him to emit a painful moan. "We're leaving, the both of us."

He gives me a weary look and collapses again onto his back. Patting my hand softly, he motions weakly with his head. "I'm not going anywhere, *ma chère*." And with that, his limb drops to the bloody leaves.

"Adrien... *Père*." I shake him, and my breath catches when I realize he's not moving, not breathing. "No, no, no..." How could this be happening? My mind goes blank until I hear a repeat of the crunching footfalls. My head whips up like a deer scenting a predator. They're here. They're coming. I lean over and place a soft kiss on Adrien's cheek, vaguely registering the already cooling temperature of his skin. "Goodbye, Adrien," I whisper, and then I'm up and moving.

From our room to check out, from the entrance of our hotel to a taxi. I think very little — focused on where I'm going and what I'll be doing. My senses are distracting, but I'm getting better at funneling the information without becoming confused. Sight, smell, hearing, taste, and touch. Each of them a pleasure and torture combined. Somehow, they heighten the sudden loss of my beloved mentor.

With a Herculean effort, I stuff these emotions in a small room of my mind and slam the door shut. *Later*, I tell myself. *Later I'll allow myself the indulgence of grief.*

I purchase my ticket at the airport, my mind unable to stop thinking about the fact that I seem destined to circle back upon myself. First back twice to London, and now back again to Italy.

In silence, I walk to my gate, sidestepping and moving through the crowd of people, each of them heading on their own adventure.

Suddenly, I'm hemmed in by men in black suits. Pushed from all sides, I instinctually grab an arm to stay upright, but then quickly release him. Where did they come from? My breath quickens and my knees tighten in a way that walking is difficult. I attempt to push at the wall of suits, but for all intents and purposes I'm caged in and being moved where they want me to go. With a mighty shove, I slam my arms into the back of the man in front of me, causing him to stumble slightly. As if it never happened, he keeps moving and doesn't break rank.

A hand from behind me grasps my arm, and with a jerk I circle on the man. Seeing the hand belongs to Eric, I stop struggling but give him a quizzical look. He keeps my arm within his grasp and moves up to walk beside me.

My mind spins. Where am I being taken?

The wall of men block out everything around me. I don't know which direction we're heading and can't see any people. The sounds of the airport mask simple conversation—it's impossible to tell if we're moving through hundreds of people or an empty corridor.

The hand on my arm shifts, and I feel Eric's thumb rubbing slowly along my skin. Electric sparks shoot from this juncture. What is he doing? Does he even know he's doing it?

A moment later, we stop and the man in front, who I pushed, opens a door. He steps to the side allowing me to proceed him through. I have no choice in the matter as the flood of black suits takes me with it into the area. The door closes behind us, and they part to reveal a well-appointed room with Stephen sitting casually in a plush chair, drinking a clear liquid. Large windows stretch the full length of the wall behind him, and beyond them, planes move to and fro.

Eric's hand tightens on my arm as I take a step. I didn't even realize I'd moved—for a moment I was consumed with a need to destroy Stephen. Adrien is dead, and whether Stephen pulled the trigger or not, he is responsible. I look from the grip on my upper arm to Eric's eyes and find my calm. His fist loosens and drops from my arm as I step forward.

"Ellen. It's so good to see you again," he says as if I have any other option but to be here.

"Stephen. What the hell is going on? Why can't you simply leave me alone?"

Standing, he walks casually toward me. "I think we're both aware that's not going to happen." With a hooded glance and a smirk in my direction, Stephen mutters, "So sorry to hear about Adrien. I guess that leaves just you and me now, hm?"

I jump forward into the room, but the men close in too quickly for me to even touch the air around him.

Shifting back into business mode, Stephen adds, "You're the Key, and I require the Key to get the information I need."

I take a deep breath and then another in an attempt to calm down; Adrien would want me to triumph by succeeding, not by putting myself in a no-win situation. *Okay. Think, Ellen. Think.* Stephen said he needs me to get information. Finally, some motive for what drives him. And from Stephen — not just speculation. "What information do you need? If I have it, I'll give it to you just to be rid of you." The sneer on my face as I say this seems to amuse him.

With a chuckle, he turns his back on me and heads to a bar along the wall. Fresh ice cubes clink into his glass and he pours himself what appears to be vodka. With a raise of his eyebrows and a gesture toward the glass, he asks if I would like a drink.

Without an answer, I turn and scan the room. There are two exits—the one we came in, and another door, which perhaps heads to the tarmac. Both avenues are blocked by large men.

"You've led me on a merry chase, Ellen." His words are complimentary and his gaze on me hungry. I can hardly stomach looking at him, and my eyes continue to survey the room. When they land on Eric, I halt the forward progression and look him straight in the eye. Perhaps this is where aid will be found. There is something there, although the look he returns is blank. Maybe *too* blank. I hold his gaze long enough to convey interest to him, but not overlong to alert Stephen.

"May I sit?"

"Of course, of course." Stephen gives another small chuckle. "Make yourself comfortable. We'll be boarding soon."

Just as I'm about to seat myself, I stop in a partial crouch, my eyes whipping to Stephen. "We? I'm not going anywhere with you."

"My men and I will be accompanying you to Vatican City, or rather, you'll be accompanying us."

Do I play dumb or just be upfront? I'm so tired of him.

"How do you know about Vatican City?"

"Haven't you figured it out yet? I know every move you make."

With a slight shift, I move into the corner of the couch and put my back to Stephen. Is he deliberately attempting to make me suspicious of Adrien? How dare he, after being the one to cause his death. But how else could he have this information, if not for him? I can't, won't believe it. What if? Damn Stephen. Damn him for putting this thought in my head.

I stare at this manipulative man. Pleased with himself, he

has a pompous grin on his face. He's way too relaxed as he sips his drink, legs crossed in front of him.

"So? What information can I give you, to get rid of you?"

As if he thinks I'm deliberately attempting to humor him, Stephen chuckles and raises his glass in a toast. "Oh, Ellen. I think we'll just tag along and see what you find."

In a low tone, a phone rings and one of the men picks up a receiver on a far table. He speaks in a soft timbre and after hanging up, walks to bend to Stephen's ear. As plain as if he's speaking directly to me, I hear the man tell Stephen the plane is ready. This increased sense of hearing may come in handy yet. After a quick nod, Stephen stands and straightens his jacket.

"Well. It appears as if our flight is ready."

When I don't immediately rise, the wall of men begins to close in on my couch. Without moving my head, my eyes scan left and right, watching them advance.

Once again, there's a hand on my arm. Startled, I glance up to see Eric looking down at me.

"Come, Ellen." His accented voice is low and he exerts gentle pressure on my arm in a lifting motion. My stomach does a slight flutter at his touch and the sound of his murmur. The deep resonance runs through my veins, and for a moment my entire being is focused on the spot where we meet. For a moment, a wonderful moment, I'm in a daze. I glance from his fingers to his eyes, and with an effort I shake off the cloud around my senses. My chin goes up and I pull my arm from his grip.

Rising to my feet, I walk slowly toward Stephen, who is staring at Eric with a confused, calculating expression on his face. I don't even want to know what he's thinking. For now, there is no choice but to acquiesce to his desires. *For now.*

Chapter 15

Throughout the couple hours it takes to fly from London to Rome, Stephen's continued attempts to engage me in conversation wear evermore at my nerves. When I realize, early on, he will tell me nothing more about the needs he mentioned, I halt any interaction between us. His voice drones on for the duration of the flight, and I don't think he even notices he is the only one talking. He so enjoys listening to himself.

Every few minutes, I can't stop myself from glancing at Eric. He sits, stoic, saying nothing. Twice, I catch his eye, and twice it's me who looks away.

Get focused, Ellen. Nothing can derail what must be.

*****

Rome. Back in Rome. Circles, flowing into each other...

By the time we arrive in Rome, the sun is setting behind the horizon. I don't know what the plan is, and no one asks my opinion. After the plane taxies to a halt on the tarmac, we exit and get in two limos. I'm placed in the first one, and most of Stephen's men take up the second. After the look on Stephen's face, it's surprising to find Eric in my limo. He and the driver sit up front while Stephen and I occupy the back. I keep my eyes open to where we are going, trying unsuccessfully to track the turns from the airport — it's a futile task, however, as I'm unfamiliar with Rome and one road looks much like another.

After an uneventful trip, all my concentration spent ignoring Stephen's attempts at conversation, we stop before a beautiful hotel. As the limo pulls under a canopy at the entrance, I catch sight of a building with multiple floors. Each room has a front balcony and each balcony is covered in flowing vines. The day is just turning to night — that wonderful, interesting time when it's both and neither. The hotel lights turn on, one by one, to magically illuminate the area. They reflect off the golden surface of the building in a blinding array that causes me to blink and look away. In the gloaming, I spot a herd of stone lions making their way across the lawn. What a curious place we've landed — it's unfortunate the company is not more to my liking.

Before the vehicle has even come to a complete halt, Eric has the front door open and reaches to open mine. What is it about him? I knew, even in the tunnels in Africa, I felt a connection with him, and he with me. With an inner snort, I recall this didn't stop me from clunking him in the head with a stone and locking him in an underground cavern. After last year, and France, I guess I've learned my lesson in trusting too soon.

The leather seats squeak as I slide to depart the limo. Stepping up the curb, large men in black once again surround me. As we pass through a set of double doors, the words *Rome Cavalieri* etched above them, I wonder if other patrons seeing us think we're very important to warrant all this protection. Little do they know, I'm just an art major from America who's in over her head.

The stunning reception area of the hotel boasts a long concierge desk with friendly, competent employees. Since art is my first love, I'm held spellbound by the works mounted on the wall behind the counter. One of Stephen's men deals quickly with the particulars as I wander to the center of the room. A large chandelier hangs from the ceiling like an inverted pyramid covered with a million lights.

"Ellen."

I turn to look at Stephen, carefully keeping my expression blank.

"Come." He reaches to grasp my elbow, but just before he can touch me, I jerk my arm away. The last thing I want is the feel of him on me. He gives me a look—a look I don't understand. Avarice. Contemplation. And perhaps a little loathing. Stephen and I have come a long way on this journey, and like mine, his emotions are complicated.

The men surround us again, Eric among them, and they usher us to an elevator. Not all of us fit, so some of them take another, but even then, I'm crushed in the press of men. For a few moments, I'm surrounded by sounds and smells of males, not all pleasant. All that is forgotten when the elevator doors pull back to reveal a hallway lined with more masterpieces. We flow out of the confines of the small box, and I make my way slowly down the corridor, stopping frequently to admire each of the paintings. Surprisingly, Stephen is patient, allowing me all the time I wish. Partway down the aisle, my attention is drawn to an open door with guards standing around. I guess this is my destination. Enough dawdling.

The room is opulent. There's no other way to put it. Gold is everywhere, and the furniture—two chaise lounges in front of a blazing fireplace—looks plush and comfy, as does the king-sized bed. My bag is set on the bed, so at least I'll be able to freshen up and change clothes. As I wander into the room, looking about, Stephen enters after me. With a spin, I turn and stare at him.

"Don't worry, Ellen. I won't be sharing a room with you…"

You bet your ass, you won't.

"…my accommodations are right across the hall, however, so if you're thinking of causing a disruption, understand, I'll know immediately."

When I continue to stare at him, saying nothing, he adds, "My men will be in the hallway and we're six stories up, so there's nowhere for you to go. Order room service and relax. We'll be heading to St. Peter's Square in the morning." This time, he doesn't wait for an answer before he turns and breezes out the door, shutting it quietly behind him.

Hustling over to it, I throw the secondary deadbolt. The last thing I need is a surprise visit from Stephen in the middle of the night. With a large sigh, I turn and lean back against the door to survey the room again. Stephen sure knows how to travel in style...

The curtains to the balcony are open, and Rome is laid out like a feast for my eyes. She glows and sparkles with lights that remind me of gems. Drawn to the sliding door, I move slowly across the room. As I near, Vatican City comes into view from the right. The dome of St. Peter's Basilica is lit, and suddenly, I realize how far from home I am and how lonely I feel. If only Adrien could be here with me to witness this.

"I'm here, Adrien. Just a little farther..."

When I reach to unlock and open the door, wishing to step out onto the balcony, a figure moves from the shadows. Stephen has been extra thorough this night. Does he think I'll rappel down six stories? With an inner shrug, I wrench the curtains closed and turn away from the vista. *Who knows, maybe I would.*

What to do? How to get away? I need to get to St. Peter's Square, and I can only imagine the problems Stephen and his men will cause. Moving to the door of the room, I pull it open, unsurprised to see the two men in suits turn and look at me. Without a word, I shut the door and lock it. *Men, men – everywhere there are men...*

Deciding to relax just a bit and let my mind ferment on my predicament, I approach the bed and rifle through my bag. I feel dirty and used up. It's been a long couple days, and I haven't had a moment to process the loss of Adrien. My fight for survival caused me to push all those emotions to the back of my mind and just function.

Grabbing some clean underclothes and something to sleep in, I head into the bathroom. *Wow!* If I thought the bedroom suite was luxurious, I'm in shock over the bathroom. Everything is gilded in gold and marble. No way around it— that huge bathtub is going to be my best friend for the next hour or so.

Laid out in the tub, watching the steam rise from the overly hot water, I consider what my next move should be. Now that I'm alone in the quiet with the comfort of the warm water, the loss of Adrien surges back to fill my head and overflow my heart. Had I done the right thing? Could I have saved him if I'd done anything differently? How will I go on without him? My breath catches, and my control breaks. Leaning forward, curling into myself within the tub, I allow myself this time to grieve. The tears are hot and painful. My sobs wrench my frame and add salt to the bath. After a time, I quiet, the tears drying, leaving me with a shaking body despite the heat of the room. Due to the powerful crying jag, I feel weakened and my eyes puffy. Splashing hot water, I wash my face and lean back against the cool marble, catching my breath.

"Okay, Adrien. I still need your direction...help me out, *père*."

The water cools and I still don't have a plan. Getting out and pulling the plug, I grab a wonderfully lavish towel and wrap myself in it. Its comfort is welcome. As though sleepwalking, I get dressed in my night clothes, turn off the lights, and climb into bed. I don't even remember my head hitting the pillow.

Chapter 16

It's midafternoon before my horde of companions and I get to St. Peter's Square. Up and ready to go before the sun rose, I don't know why it took so long for Stephen to show up, and when he did, I was given no explanation. The delay afforded me the opportunity to partake in some of the most excellent fare I've had the good fortune to taste. My stomach is pleasantly full, and my mind is set. This day will end my journey — one way or the other.

St. Peter's Square is magnificent.

The sun is past its zenith and beginning its decent to the horizon. The Square is full of people, the faithful and the tourists. Mixing with the citizens, keeping an eye on them, are members of the Swiss Guard. Their brightly colored, striped uniforms stand out among the press of people. Covertly, I watch one such garbed young man walk by, noting the sword attached to a belt at his waist. He and the other soldiers will be another obstacle I'll need to deal with.

As I stand, my brain can't even process the image of the wheel that is St. Peter's Square. The surface is marked by eight spokes, and in the center an obelisk stands, reaching toward the sky. My needle. Gazing at the stone structure in the hub of the Square, I'm reminded of another obelisk, another time. The excitement and fear that night in Paris with James. A small shudder moves through my frame at the memory of what followed that evening's flight. Scanning up and up at the monolith, a sigh escapes my lips, and I note this column is taller than the one in Paris.

And now look at where I am. I hope I won't be required to climb this one.

Strolling across the Square, I attempt to ignore my tail of four of Stephen's men. On either side of the obelisk are matching three-tier fountains. The sound of gurgling water as it cascades down from the top tier is comforting in an odd way. It's at one of them where I stop and rest, getting a good look at the entire area. With curiosity, I move forward toward the obelisk to stand on a metal disk embedded within the ground. It's one of two ellipse points within St. Peter's Square. Pivoting slowly in a stationary circle, I'm astonished to see for myself that from this spot the four rows of columns of the colonnades fall perfectly, one behind the other, to appear as if only one row exists. Incredible architecture for the 1600s.

Now that my mind has relaxed and stopped thinking

frantically, I'm able to truly see the Square. Why didn't I notice this before? With the setting of the sun, a shadow is being cast by the obelisk. With every moment, the shadow reaches farther and farther, looking more and more like a compass needle, pointing...but to what?

Square but not square;
in the closing, a needle shall point the way.
Laid at her foothold, a circle is created and the Key opens a gate.
The new guard plays eternal.

The clue plays over in my head. Is this the needle pointing the way? And does the closing mean the ending of the day? Sunset?

Obviously I'm showing too much interest in the obelisk and its shadow, because Stephen walks up. "What do you see, Ellen? What has caught your interest so intensely?"

My brows pull together in a scowl as I look his way. "Fuck off, Stephen," I say, deadpan, and walk away from him. My frown deepens when I hear his chuckle behind me.

Strolling, attempting to keep it casual, I wander my way around the Square. Up above, on the top of the colonnades, are statues of saints. They encircle the area, looking down on the faithful. Continuing to look everywhere and nowhere, I approach the location where the shadow of the obelisk points. It's at the open end of the colonnades, and there are four possible statues in this space. I need the sun to lower just a bit more for the point of the shadow to define which statue it wants.

Daughter...

The voice reverberates in my head. My footsteps falter,

and I scan the area for the source.

Daughter…

I move forward, wondering at the voice. As I walk by the area in question, planning on taking a lap around the Square, a realization pierces my brain, something I saw but didn't comprehend. With a break in my stride, I stop, thinking, then glance back at the statues on the end. Step by step, I continue my walk. I was right! A surge of energy flows through my system, and my heart thumps a frantic beat. Of the statues in the correct location, only one of them is a woman. *Laid at her foothold… Laid at* her *foothold.* The female statue must be who I'm looking for. Is it she who spoke to me? Now, how to lose Stephen and his men? They're monitoring every move I make.

I open my senses and take a good long look around. The sun will soon be down—I'm out of time. I need to get to the roof and to the statue of the saint.

From the center of the Square up to the steps leading into St. Peter's Basilica, waist-high fences corral the people and lead them where they need to go. Closer to the buildings, chairs are set up for the outside service. I throw a leg over the fencing and again over the next one to move quickly toward the Basilica. Already, a commotion is beginning behind me. Glancing over my shoulder, I see some of Stephen's men heading my way. Stephen is nowhere in sight. His men move on an interception trajectory, but some are also coming from the other side. They hope to create a cage and force me back. As I come to an opening in the chairs, I break into a sprint, straight for the entry to the Basilica. I don't know where to go, but I need to get to the roof of the colonnade and to the statue of the female saint.

Even though I tell myself to not look back, keep moving

forward, I can't stop from glancing behind me again. The commotion of men rushing forward has alerted the Swiss Guard, and now they join in the ruckus. They appear to be more curious than worried for the time being. People around the Square have stopped to watch the excitement. It's plain by their faces they are interested, not concerned.

Suddenly, a shot rings out. Everyone in the Square ducks, dropping to their knees—myself included. I scan the area, swinging my head from side to side, trying to locate where the shot came from. I feel my heart leaping in my chest and breathing deep, I try to quiet my senses.

One of Stephen's men—and the only person standing—has a gun in his hand. How in the world did he get it past the security checkpoint? And why is he shooting? Through none of this have I thought Stephen wanted me dead, and I still don't. This guy better hope the Swiss Guard gets to him before Stephen does. Standing, I run up the stairs, taking them two at a time. Another shot sounds and a bullet whizzes by my ear. Wrenching to the side, but still running, I reach the door and glance back to see the Swiss Guard tackling the idiot with the gun. I'd like to kiss him for creating such a wonderful diversion. Maybe the Guard will be so preoccupied with him, they won't notice me.

With a large push, I muscle open the door just as an arm grabs me from behind, spinning me around. Eric. Where did he come from? I haven't seen him all afternoon. But I have no time to waste. I need to get to the saint. Over his shoulder, I see the furor of the pile of Swiss Guards, but around them, moving swiftly, are other black-suited men, heading my way. I push past Eric and continue, looking frantically for access to the colonnades and ultimately the roof.

"Ellen."

His husky murmur sends hot chills down my spine, causing me to stiffen. Spinning around, I give him a dirty look. I don't need this distraction—not now, not when I'm so close.

"I'm busy," I whisper and point my finger into his chest.

"Allow me to help you."

His face is earnest, his eyes honest and clear, and really, I can use all the help I can get.

"I need to get onto the roof of the colonnade."

He wastes a few seconds processing this information, staring at me, unblinking. Then he takes my hand and turns toward a hall with multiple doors. Just as we turn into the hall, the front door of the Basilica is thrown open and a sea of black suits flows in. I catch a fleeting glance at them, but due to the wall they don't immediately see us. Eric tries one door to find it locked. Continuing down the hall, he grabs another knob, which turns easily. Opening the door, with his hand on the small of my back, he urges me through. The corridor beyond is dark, and not knowing what's ahead of me, I stand still. A light comes on overhead, allowing me to see Eric's hand on the switch. The illumination reveals a short hallway with a flight of stairs at the end. It's there that he leads me, and together we climb the stairs.

The thought that I may be acting the dupe enters my head, but I've decided to trust him and until he breaks that trust, I'll hold to it.

At the top of the stairs are three doors—one on each side of the landing and one directly in front of us. Without hesitation, Eric opens the right door and ushers us through. When the light comes on, we're in a service room with equipment and tools laid out. Stepping forward, he advances into the recesses of the room, and only when we get near the wall do I make out the outline of an access panel.

A feeling of dizziness makes me sway as my breathing comes fast and hard. This is it. All this time and work and loss, and the end is before me.

With one last searching look at me, Eric unlatches the panel and pushes it open into the late evening air. He places one foot outside and reaches for me. With my hand in his, I enter the panel and make to move past him, our bodies sliding by each other. He stops me easily with an open palm on my cheek, using his thumb to tip my head up to look at him. My heart beats a wild rhythm in my ears, and all I see is his eyes. Slowly, his head lowers toward mine. For the moment, I've forgotten my quest in the sensation of his breath on my skin and the anticipation of his kiss. With a hair's breadth between us, there's a mighty crash outside the door, and both our heads spin to look. Voices can be heard. Frantic voices coming our way.

"Go. Do what you must."

With a look at him, I nod and turn out the doorway. He steps onto the roof with me, swinging the panel shut and blocking it with his large body. If there's enough of them, even that won't hold, but it may give me the time I need.

At the end of the day, the light is peculiar and traversing the roof precarious. Statues and stone sidewalls cast shadows over the red tile, making it difficult to see the walkway between the pitch of the roof and the edge where the statues stand. The figures are huge, reaching almost ten feet tall, and are spaced about that far apart. Lights from within the plaza are just coming up to illuminate the area. The view of the dome of St. Peter's Basilica makes me catch my breath. This is certainly a sight not many people have the opportunity to see. With another glance down, I spot Stephen in the middle of a mix of people: his men, the Swiss Guard, and random tourists. As if he's felt my gaze, his eyes shift up and lock on me. His lips move, and I read my name on them, but I'm too far to hear him. Swinging from me, he pushes people for access across the Square. I watch him for a moment and then turn. He'll never reach me in time.

Partway along the roof, a large *bang* sounds. I glance about to see Eric's body thrown backwards as the door to the panel flies open and the distinctive uniforms of the Swiss Guard fill the area. Even in the fading light, the colorful yellow, blue, and red stripes are clearly visible. With one hand on a statue, I watch as Eric scrambles up to engage the Guard. The odds are overwhelmingly in their favor, but for a moment he holds his own. As they engulf him, he turns toward me and retreats onto the roof, blocking their way. The skirmish comes farther down the colonnade, moving closer to my position.

Picking up my speed, I hasten to the end of the roof. Just past a large likeness of a coat of arms, on the very corner, is my saint.

Daughter…

The voice fills my head again, only louder this time. Glancing up at the marble statue, I see she has a slight shimmer.

Laid at her foothold.

Dropping to my knees at the base of the statue, I pull my bag from my back. With no time for finesse, I upend it and pour the contents out beside me. Within the mess of objects, is the box holding the tokens I've collected. With a rough grab, I pull it from the rest, shoving the remaining items aside. Pushing up my sleeve, I pull the band from my arm.

The sound of fighting has me giving a hasty look over my shoulder, only to see the group of men closer than ever. My time is up.

Wrenching open the box, I gaze down at the objects inside, my memories pouring forth. The trials that were met to claim them—the losses incurred. Reverently but quickly, I take them out one by one and place them in a circle at the foot of the saint.

The leaf. Buddha the enlightened one.

The gold weight. Anansi the trickster.

The Wheel of Fortune tarot card. The goddess Fortuna.

The wooden tiles. Garuda.

The silver armband. A triad of granite men.

As all things in this quest, they are now in an eternal circle, a wheel. Reaching up, I unclasp my medallion from around my neck, pulling the chain out and dropping it. Staring down at the metal piece, memories again assault my brain. My parents gifting me with it—and me having claimed it years before. Spending the greatest length of my life wearing it. It becoming a part of me.

In the last light of the setting sun, the metal is reflected, and I see what I didn't notice before. Red. Dried blood from Adrien. His last contribution to this cause. His blood on my amulet.

I glance once more at Eric to see he's lost his battle with the Guard. They have him on the ground, hands held behind his back while more of their company swarm over him, heading toward me. Our eyes lock for one final time, and I have a second of "what ifs." I'll miss this man.

The sun sinks below the horizon, and a final streak of light impacts with the medallion as I set it in the center of the circle — the hub of the wheel.

A brilliance erupts from the inside of the amulet like a nova exploding. In absolute, perfect silence, I'm bathed in its glory. For what seems an eternity, all I know is the light. As it begins to retract, running back into the center of the medallion, my body becomes a million molecules and I'm part of the light, traveling, traveling...

Chapter 17

Behind the mask, the Guardian opens steel-gray eyes for the first time, her essence as Ellen Thompson a fading memory. The hopes, fears, dreams, and phobias of the human existence a thing of the past. Her slate is clean, and all she knows is this vista around her.

Above, the open sky is filled with lights. When she tips her head back and looks, the lights become worlds, each beautiful and unique in its own right. With concentration, she realizes she can see farther and farther, closer and closer to each world. This is her vocation, her calling.

Attention back on the gathering, she sees them all: the trickster, the goddess, the warrior, them and many more. A pattern of beings—moving in an eternal circle. Taking a moment to watch, she registers a feeling of contentment, of coming home. With a new purpose, the Guardian steps forward and takes her place in the immortal cycle.

*****

With a flexing, like the bursting of a bubble on a still lake, a displacement alters the pattern of time and space. On a variety of worlds, a small change takes place. A change hardly noticeable. Five tokens and the catalyst for them, a metallic medallion, appear. Each hidden, each waiting. Waiting for their time to again come. For a Guardian to be called.

Epilogue

MANY YEARS LATER…

The wail of a healthy newborn, vibrating through the village, causes more than a few grins of relief and happiness. It's been a long, hard labor, the coming of a new babe a blessing for the people.

A village elder — the grandfather of the child — moves to the hut where the sleeping mother and infant lie. He's waited most of his life for this moment. He has what the ancients called "the sight" as did his father and his father before him. Will this child be the one he waits for?

With a drop of his head, he moves through the entry and stands looking at the swaddle of cloths. Straining his ears, he perceives the deep breaths of the resting child. With apprehension and determination filling his every cell, he moves forward to unwrap the blankets. His breath escapes him as awe and relief fill the void. For just a moment, he sees a shining aura around the infant, but in the next blink, it's gone. It was enough.

With ancient hands, the elder lifts a necklace from his own neck to place it around the babe's. On the leather band is a medallion, timeless and beautiful. It has strange etchings and a hole in the middle.

The game begins.

Acknowledgments

I would like to thank Big Bus Tours of London, England, and their employee Phil Harris, Sightseeing Administrator, for identifying the sculpture *A World Beyond* by Ernest Cole. Without their assistance, the scene at County Hall in London couldn't have taken place.

Also, to Laura Callender and Crystal MM Burton of JustPublishIt.com for the cover art and editing. Thanks for your talent and time, ladies!

Made in the USA
Coppell, TX
14 September 2022

83113717R10136